For William and Cheryl;
They know why.

KILLING HELEN

Sarah Challis

HEADLINE

First published in Great Britain in 2000 by
HEADLINE BOOK PUBLISHING

10 9 8 7 6 5 4 3 2 1

British Library Cataloguing in Publication Data

Challis, Sarah
Kiling Helen
I.Title
823.9'14[F]

ISBN 0 7472 7236 0

Typeset by Letterpart Ltd
Reigate, Surrey

Printed and bound in Great Britain by
Mackays of Chatham

HEADLINE BOOK PUBLISHING
A division of Hodder Headline
338 Euston Road
London NW1 3BH
www.headline.co.uk
www.hodderheadline.com

Chapter One

For some time I have been planning to murder Helen. It will be a traceless crime, that is the beauty of it. There will be absolutely nothing to link her to me. My name does not appear in her diary or address book. No neighbour will recall a woman of my description at her door. Helen, of course, does not know of my existence – and it is this that gives me my power over her and will make my crime possible. Robert is another matter altogether – 'a horse of a very different colour', to use one of his expressions. He will quickly be drawn into police enquiries.

I imagine him having to tell Mary, his wife, that he has to go with the officers to the police station to answer some questions. Mary will look up from a seed catalogue, her customary expression of detachment for once lifted into curiosity. 'What on earth for? The *police station*?' It makes me smile to think of it. The smooth surface of his well-ordered life will be ruffled and disturbed. He will have some explaining to do.

There are all sorts of technical problems about how actually to get hold of Helen, lure her down here to my cottage in Somerset to give me the opportunity of smashing her head in with a brick, running her over, or pushing her off Alfred's Tower, our 160-foot local land-mark. I thought of this possibility at Easter as I viewed, with knees trembling from the climb and the height, distant Longleat and the landmarks of three counties. She would sail through the air, her mouth open in surprise, her beautiful and thoughtful clothes filled with rushing air, her expensive London haircut of no help to her now in her headlong fall to the ground below.

I'd decided against stabbing. I didn't like the idea of spurting blood and I wasn't convinced that I'd be able to plunge a knife into warm and living flesh. Pushing or bashing were a possibility. The other day when I telephoned her I found her intonation particularly annoying. She says, 'Haylo?' and her voice is little and feminine. I much prefer Mary, who barks, 'HaLow?' with all the emphasis on the second syllable, as if you are interrupting something important. Anyway, I put the receiver down as usual. Just checking. Helen enjoys embroidery and since her husband finally divorced her a year ago, she plays bridge in the afternoons and has taken up golf. If I had to make a list of things I would most hate to do, these three would be at the top. We are so different, you see. All Helen's occupations require patience, refinement, careful thought and consideration, whilst I go at things with a rush and a clamour. Tortoise and hare – and I know very well who won that particular race.

All this I think about in the soft summer nights. I live so far away from other habitation that a car passing at night along my lane wakes me and I lie in the velvety darkness with the curtains breathing at the open cottage window and I plot Helen's death. Having murder in my heart does not mean that I am unhappy. Far from it. This past year at Jerusalem Farm has been good. I love it in the country and, for the most part, do not miss London at all. I get whiffs of the old life when I talk to my cousin, Loops, or my old friend, Poppy, but I don't envy them the King's Road or night clubs or places where you can buy *panettone*. At the village shop here we are very much restricted to sliced white bread and tinned peas. Nothing more foreign than the occasional grapefruit. I've done what my mother, Anne, calls settling down. She is almost proud of me. I rent this pretty cottage, have a dog, and teach the violin at a well-known local girls' school. All quite satisfactory except for one thing.

I am thirty-two and unmarried.

Robert can't really be blamed. We are the architects of our own fate and no one could say I wasn't warned. My Robert thoughts I tend to keep for the morning when the murderous ones of the night are dispelled by the sun twinkling on the wet grass as I let Pilgrim out into the garden. Pilgrim is a gentle brindle greyhound, abandoned when he got too old and slow, and collected by me from a rescue home when I moved to the cottage. He now looks much less like a twist of rusted wire and there is flesh on his ribs. He is inscrutable and trusting and lays his long muzzle on my knee and gazes into my face with his toffee-coloured eyes, ready to love again those who had treated him so cruelly.

As Pilgrim picks his way delicately through the dew to his favoured bush, and the bricks by the back door are warm on my toes, I make my early cup of tea in a special bone china cup and saucer Robert once bought me from a Paris antiques market. These small ceremonies are important to me in these solitary days and, collecting a biscuit for Pilgrim, we go back up to bed, Pilgrim's bunched, racing haunches sloping up the steep stairs in front of me.

I allow him onto the bed and he lies like a warm log, sighing with pleasure. Where is Robert waking? I imagine him stretching and grunting, farting too. He is never embarrassed by the mechanics of his body. He is, if nothing else, comfortable with himself. Sometimes I run my hands down my own flanks, feeling my skin soft and silky. This is what he would feel. But of course, it isn't the same and only arouses a sense of loss.

<hr />

3

If anyone helped it start, apart from me, it was Poppy. Five years ago, she and I were playing in a string orchestra in a dismal disused cinema in an unfashionable part of North London, somewhere like Burnt Oak and there he was in the audience. Robert is a very large man and his head towered above the small crowd; he is always noticeable because of his height and his Roman Emperor looks. He wears his hair rather long and that night I noticed how it swept straight back to curl on the collar of his expensive overcoat.

Poppy knew him. He came over to talk to us after the performance and was kind and amusing. He asked me how I was managing financially, as people often do of young professional musicians, and I said, 'Not very well,' and told him about a grant I was applying for, to play in Northern Ireland. He wondered if he could help and handed me his business card.

'Give me a ring,' he said, and looked into my eyes a little too long. I knew this later as a knack he has. It makes people feel he is especially interested in them and invites reckless confidences from women.

'Thanks,' I said, turning the card over in my hand.

He smiled and held my eyes again. 'Have you any idea of the effect of a beautiful young woman playing the violin?'

Later I told this to Poppy as we stood in the street waiting for Chris, Poppy's husband, to collect us. I dug his card out of my coat pocket. She snorted. 'You are pathetic, Harriet Lennox. Flattery will get anyone everywhere with you! You're on to a good one there though. Robert Mackintosh is on the Arts Council and a Director of the Royal Academy. He's chairman of the music publishers – you know, Mackintosh's, the same name. Old family business. My father knows him quite well.' Poppy's father was a distinguished horn player.

'Married?'

'Of course. Never see his wife, though – he's always

on his own. He's very attractive, isn't he, for a man of his age. Give him a ring, for God's sake. Prostitute yourself for Art. You'd make him a lovely mistress.'

I laughed because she was joking.

I put his card beside my bed and looked at it often but waited three days before I telephoned him. Then I spoke to a very chilly secretary who said he was in a meeting. When I asked if he could ring me back, she took my number and managed to convey by her tone that she would screw it up and throw it in the bin the moment I put the receiver down.

Feeling ridiculously nervous, as if I was anticipating something momentous, I hung around for a while until the silence in my flat became overpowering and oppressive and I could not ignore the telephone as it crouched, obstinately refusing to ring. Finally, using a technique that often works, I ran a hot scented bath and was forcing myself to lie back in the foam when the telephone rang.

It was Robert. His voice sounded wonderful – deep and dark brown. He was assured and confident and relaxed. I could feel my heart beating in my throat as I stood naked talking to him, my feet leaving wet prints on the Oxfam rug made in a co-operative in some remote Indian village. It seemed he had telephoned several people on my account and had some helpful suggestions to make.

'Look,' he said, 'would you like to meet me for lunch? How about Wednesday?' He sounded as if he was flicking through a diary.

'Yes, of course, I'd love to. Where?' We arranged to meet at Covent Garden.

Just at the point when our conversation had come to an end, he said, 'What are you wearing?'

I giggled nervously. 'Nothing, as it happens. I was in the bath.'

A pause.

'Oh God!' he said, and rang off.

I telephoned Poppy immediately.

'He wants a London bonk,' she said.

'Do you think so? He's so *nice*. Why can't I meet uncomplicated men? I don't need an old married man like him.'

'Come round,' said Poppy. I could hear her baby, Jess, screaming in the background. 'I'm so fed up with this fucking baby.'

We both laughed. Poppy loved Jess to distraction. She had been married then for four years to Chris, a banker, who was pink and fair and straightforward, and who loved Poppy for her wild tumbling black hair, her exotic slanting eyes and her precarious profession as a violinist. No one at the time could think what Poppy saw in him, but I knew. He represented a good stake in bricks and mortar. He had insurance policies and a shiny company car. He took the world seriously and was thoroughly grown up. He was exactly what Poppy needed as the father of her child.

'Okay,' I said. 'I'll come now.' I got dressed in a tight skirt and a silly cotton gypsy top and put on high velvet heels. I painted my mouth scarlet. I felt dangerous and very, very sexy. However, on my way down my dirty hot street I twice fell off the heels and made some workmen laugh. I gave them the finger. I stopped at the off-licence and bought a bottle of cold white wine and a chocolate Easter egg for Jess which I realised was a mistake as soon as I was out in the hot street again.

It was warm and stuffy on the Tube and gusts of hot wind blew down the tunnels. I teetered along Poppy's road, past the derelict houses to the up-and-coming end where the doors had been painted and sash windows lovingly restored. Poppy had the upper three floors of such a house. Chris had sandblasted and painted everything in hot Mediterranean colours. It looked lovely today, filled with sunshine. Jess had fallen asleep and lay just wearing a nappy, her hair damp with sweat, one tiny clenched fist on her chest, the other arm flung out to the side.

'Oh Pops, she's gorgeous,' I said. 'I want a baby just like her. I want one this afternoon, right now.'

'No, you don't, you fool,' said Poppy. She looked exhausted, with plum-coloured rings under her eyes. 'God, I envy you. I've forgotten what it's like to be free.'

'Not very nice, really,' I said. 'I long to be the reason someone hurries home from work. I'd hold our lovely baby up at the window as Daddy came down the street.'

Poppy groaned. 'All Chris hurries home for is sex. He seems to think of nothing else, while I've gone off it completely.'

I'd heard Poppy make this type of remark quite a lot recently. She looked so lovely, slim again after the baby; with her long legs and beautiful smooth brown skin, it seemed to me no wonder Chris felt like he did. I knew, however, that I was supposed to sympathise.

'I lie there trying really hard to think of something else. Sometimes I try and name the counties of England, alphabetically, or the stops on the Circle Line.'

'Poor Chris,' I said.

'What about me? Poor me, you mean. Honestly, Harriet, I can't bear it. All that humping, and all the pretending. I can't stand being squashed and the breathing in my ear. I feel too tired. I just want my body to myself.'

'God! I can't imagine feeling like that,' I said.

'I can quite believe it, because sex is still fun for you. A recreation, not a duty.'

'You do make married life seem like a sentence.'

'No, of course it's not. Lots of it is lovely. What I'd really prefer is just to be cosy. To cuddle on the sofa – but oh no, that won't do. It's five minutes of sex and then on with the television, get a beer out of the fridge. It's just feeding another appetite. Everyone says I feel

7

like I do because of having a baby and that I'll get over it. I just hope that happens before I know the entire London Underground system off by heart. I actually go and sneak off sometimes and look up what comes after where I've got stuck, like what station is after South Kensington.'

'I think that's worse than having a beer,' I said.

'Probably is,' said Poppy.

Change of subject. 'What am I going to wear?' I asked. 'What do you think his wife is like?'

'I think she's very elegant with well-cut and rinsed hair . . . blonde now she's going grey. I think she wears really expensive classic clothes. And good jewellery. She could afford it, and they live in Scotland so she'll be tweedy or plaidy – you know, with brooches and Celtic stuff. So you will have to look young and funky. What have you got that isn't derelict and ethnic?'

'Nothing,' I said. 'You know I look like a bag lady.'

'Well, you don't today. Wear what you've got on today.'

'I can't. He'll think I'm a tart.'

'Well, you are. Anyway, men of his age, with wives, they like tarty girls. They have all the well-bred, good-taste stuff at home.'

We opened the wine I'd brought and because Poppy didn't want to disturb Jess by taking her down to the garden, a sooty square bravely planted with geraniums in pots, we drank it in the kitchen, sitting with our legs out of the first-floor window. Poppy's were miles slimmer and browner than mine, so it was a bit depressing, but I cheered myself up by thinking of how he'd called me beautiful.

We sat and talked and laughed and when Jess woke up I held her hot little body on my lap and gave her a mug of juice. Her fair hair was damp in the delicious scoop at the base of her neck, which seemed as fragile as a flower's stalk. Poppy made us tea and then we dressed

8

Jess and pushed her down the road to the supermarket to get salami and tomatoes for supper. When we got back, the telephone was ringing and it was Chris saying he would be late and wouldn't want feeding. Poppy was very curt with him on the telephone and I wondered how marriages could contain such hostility.

'Why do you sound so cross?' I asked.

'Because I'm fed up with him,' said Poppy. 'He comes and goes as if I'm a bloody servant.' She threw herself into an armchair. 'I don't care anyway. Stay and have some supper.' So I did. We drank some more wine and when Chris got home, looking rumpled and tired, we were noisy and Poppy's mood had changed again for the better, although she looked exhausted. He kissed us both in turn, me first, and asked what we were celebrating.

'Hazzy's found a man,' said Poppy.

Stupidly, I almost felt I had. It was fun denying it and laughing as Chris asked questions. And that's how it began. As a bit of a laugh.

Chapter Two

I felt nervy with excitement about Wednesday's lunch although I tried to remind myself that it was quite legitimate and that my naughty aspirations were only in my head: nothing need happen to turn them into reality. Half of me argued that a married man was no good to me. I wonder now that I had no feelings for his wife, but somehow I refused to consider her position other than if she let such an attractive man loose she was careless and got what she deserved. I feel ashamed of that now. It puts me in the same camp as Helen.

Half of me believed that I had built the whole thing up and that there was nothing beneath the surface of his teasing, flirtatious remarks. At other times it seemed that I was sailing towards an iceberg . . . a small glittering white shape above the water, while below there was a fatal mass waiting to change the course of my life for ever.

Anyway, I took a lot of trouble over my appearance. It took me all the morning to get ready and in the end I discarded my tart's outfit, and wore a pair of tight white jeans and a deliberately shrunken yellow cashmere cardigan. I am a tall girl, a 'big girl', rather a Nordic type, I like to think. People mistakenly expect me to have been good at sport at school, whereas I spent most games afternoons hiding in the boiler-house under the swimming pool, smoking with my other layabout friends.

Dressed like this, I felt younger and fresher and more alluring to an older man. Casual, fit, sexy. I undid some buttons and wore a maximum uplift bra. I painted my toenails and chose a simple pair of flat sandals that someone had left in my flat after a party. They were expensive. I think they must have been Loops's booty after some modelling assignment.

I kept looking at my watch and trying to work out how long it would take me to get to the restaurant he'd chosen in Covent Garden. Much later, I found out that Helen had taken him there and that it was a regular haunt of theirs. Too anxious to be coolly late I arrived too early. I wanted a pee but didn't dare go in before him, and when I stared in the door, two or three waiters sprang forward and put me off. It was the sort of place where they wear napkins draped over their arms and hover about menacingly. I read the menu outside which was written in that especially French loopy writing and noticed that it was very expensive. I was just contemplating going to look for a Ladies when a taxi drew up and there he was, smiling and gesturing at the window and then getting out, head first as big men do, like bulls getting to their feet.

I stood back on the pavement while he thanked and paid the driver and exchanged remarks about Scotland in a very chummy way. Later I knew this easy charm and saw it worked on so many people that it became an annoyance. No wonder Mary grew gruff and monosyllabic. How could anyone compete with this disarming niceness?

He turned to me and held my arms while he scanned my face with special attention, again a fraction longer than was entirely comfortable, then kissed me on both cheeks and made an 'Mmmm' noise. 'You smell wonderful,' he said, 'and look good enough to eat.' He drew his fingers up the soft sleeve of my cardigan and looked into my eyes as he did so.

When he led the way in, the head waiter appeared and with more exchanged pleasantries showed us to a table and pulled out my chair. We settled ourselves and Robert had a good look at all the other diners before putting on reading glasses and studying the wine list. He was so grown-up and assured. I sat quietly, still wanting to go to the loo but not seeing any sign of one.

'What are you going to eat?' he asked. 'I can recommend this, or this.' He pointed to the menu. Helen's dishes, no doubt, I realise now.

'Yes, lovely. I mean, anything. I love all food.'

He laughed. 'How refreshing. Most girls nibble lettuce.'

'Not me. This may be the only meal I get this week,' I joked.

'Surely things are not as bad as that?' he asked.

'No, of course not. But the summer is always a bit flat.'

And then we talked and I flirted outrageously and squeezed my arms to my sides so my breasts roosted together and watched his gaze drawn to them as I knew it would be. We had a huge lunch and I ate and drank everything that he put before me and he loved feeding me, I could tell.

As I sipped a brandy he very gently traced my hand with a finger and, slightly drunk, I asked, 'Where is this taking us?'

'I think that's rather up to you, my dear. I've enjoyed your company very much indeed and will certainly do what I can to help you. As for anything else, I'm a married man and intend to stay that way, and I don't believe in love affairs. Passion, yes – but not love. If you wanted a lustful friendship with me, that would be wonderful. But it is entirely up to you,' and he took a sip of brandy and looked into my eyes.

'God!' I said. 'You're terribly cool and matter-of-fact about it.'

'Not at all,' he smiled. 'My middle-aged heart is beating rather rapidly. In case you believe otherwise, it is unusual for me to have a beautiful young woman appear to want me. I lead a very sedate life.'

I was half-drunk and relaxed and felt very sexy. I found him hugely attractive. His largeness. His authority. The fact that when he paid the bill he did so with a platinum credit card. All shallow of me, I know, but I am being honest and you need to remember that I was used to a life of relative poverty, of paying my way with equally bankrupt boyfriends, so there is some excuse for my head being so easily turned. He was also disarming, a very good listener but a talker too, so that I felt that he had enjoyed my company as much as I had his.

The waiters were polite and deferential, paying me special attention. As we left the manager said as he held the door, 'Monsieur is a very lucky gentleman.'

'Indeed!' said Robert, smiling and taking my arm in a courtly fashion.

Outside, the London pavements were hot and crowded. The afternoon light glared down and glittered on the hard surfaces of cars and tarmac. I looked at my watch. It was 3.45. It seemed an hour of the day with endless possibilities. I can swear that I had no idea of what was going to happen; I was entirely in his hands.

Robert took my arm and hailed a taxi. He held the door open and I got in. He followed and we sped off. I didn't catch what he said to the driver.

'Where now?' I asked as I leant back on the hot seat. Robert took my hand.

'A violinist's fingers,' he said, 'and strong wrists. A lovely arm,' he pushed back the neck of my cardigan, 'and a lovely shoulder.' He kissed me beside my bra strap, before gently pulling it down. Oh God! I can remember it now. How that first physical contact made me feel turned to water, dissolved by desire.

'We're going to my club,' he said, 'where I now stay when I am in London. It's not a very smart one, more for

14

country bumpkins like me and their wives. We can have a drink, a cup of tea if you'd like it, and then decide what to do. Have you anywhere you need to be?'

'In bed with you,' I said.

The next part was a routine which eventually became familiar. There was the tension of collecting his key and getting me swiftly into the lift – huge and clanking with heavy folding metal doors – and then along a dim corridor and into a rather dull dark room, with two single beds. It could have been night-time. The draped window looked out onto a deep well between tall buildings. It was miles from being seductive.

'It's a bit spartan, I'm afraid,' said Robert as I looked around. 'Had I known any of this was going to happen I would have chosen something with a little more ambience.'

'No. It's fine,' I said.

He drew me towards him and gently unbuttoned my cardigan and pulled it off my shoulders. 'Mmm, lovely breasts.' He slid my bra straps down and then his hands moved to my back and he deftly undid the hooks. My naked breasts looked good. I could see them in the glass of the dressing table. He stroked them and cupped them and rolled my nipples in his fingers, before leaning his head down to take each one in turn into his mouth. I ran my fingers through his hair, which was soft and clean. I undid his tie and some of his shirt buttons while he busied himself with my jeans which were tight and difficult to undo. I worried about the roll of fat that he'd be feeling above the waistband.

'Here, I'll do that,' I offered, and pulled them off. This left me standing in my pants, which I have to say I'd chosen quite carefully, but even so I felt shy and climbed into one of the beds and pulled the sheet up. He meanwhile finished undressing and was busy folding his trousers over a chair. I had to make myself not laugh, especially as he was only wearing boxer shorts and socks. Completely unabashed he pulled off his remaining clothes and turned to get into bed with me. His cock was huge. Not particularly long but tremendously thick. And that was it. We had a wonderful afternoon of sex and he was a truly great and considerate lover. Afterwards when we lay together in that washed-up time after sex, he was gentle and sweet but I felt that terrible sadness which invades the spirit when sexual excitement wears off. The whole afternoon had been like a dream but in a moment we would have to get up, shower, fumble into our clothes and exchange everyday remarks. He would kiss me goodbye and it would be over.

Casual afternoon sex.

'What are you thinking of?' he asked as I lay in his arms.

'Just how this makes me feel sad,' I said.

'Ah,' he said. 'The price of sex without love.'

'Won't you love me a bit?' I asked, stung that he should choose this moment to remind me of the limits of what he had offered.

'Alas, no,' he said. 'I shall think of you fondly, and lustfully, of course, but no, I won't love you. I did warn you of that.'

'Do you love your wife?' I asked.

'No. I'm not sure I ever have. We live in a fairly affectionate and companionable way. She has been a wonderful mother and I will never leave her. Sex isn't good . . . never was, particularly.'

'So do you have a lot of girlfriends?'

'No, my dear, certainly not. I have a long-standing friend I see about every three months. In the past I had numerous relationships which one way or the other hurt Mary very much. I am careful now to protect her and she chooses not to find out.'

'So is my name going to be added to a list?' I persisted.

He laughed. 'Don't be naughty or I'll spank you. If

16

you want to know, you will be my only London girlfriend, if indeed that is what you choose to be.'

'Yes, please,' I said, 'and spank me anyway.'

We said goodbye in Robert's room, for I was going down in the lift first to avoid any embarrassing encounters with other Members. He held me in his arms and kissed me tenderly.

'You're so solid,' he said.

'What? Thanks very much!'

'It's a compliment. You are a big strong girl and I find that very attractive.'

This seemed to me like backtracking. I did not like this word 'solid'. It was too much like 'hefty' and all the other adjectives used to describe tall, broad-shouldered, wide-hipped women. I thought about this all the way home to my flat, and took the opportunity to look at myself in shop windows. Solid. The afternoon felt spoiled. I'd let him see me naked and had twisted and turned with him on the single bed, and all the time he'd been thinking how big I was. What a bloody thing to say. I felt hurt and angry. He was a large man himself, but how typically male that he felt he could make that remark to me. I'd laughed afterwards and pretended that I didn't mind and he'd kissed me again and said that he would be away for a few weeks but would telephone me when he was again in London.

When I got back I made myself an enormous cheese and mayonnaise sandwich. I was a large size 14, and at my height that seemed all right. Not gross or overweight. I took all my clothes off and having no full-length mirror, stood and looked at bits of me that I could see reflected in the glass of the bathroom cupboard. Yes, I was, well, substantial.

I telephoned Poppy but Chris answered the telephone.

'Chris, would you call me solid?'

'Thick, do you mean?'

17

'No. Not intellectually. Am I large, Chris? Would you call me hefty? Tell me honestly.'

'You are deliciously curvaceous,' he said diplomatically.

'Huh!' I said.

Loops was asleep when I telephoned her.

'Loops, would you call me solid?'

'What?' she mumbled. 'Shit!' and I could hear something being knocked over.

'Solid, Loops. Would you say I was solid?'

's-o-i-l-e-d?' said Loops, who is dyslexic.

'Fat,' I said.

'Yeah. You are. Now fuck off and let me sleep.'

Chapter Three

I have lived here in Somerset for a year. It seemed the right thing to do, to move out of London. I had been thinking for some time of looking for a teaching job, but didn't fancy lion-taming in a London school. Idly flicking through the *Times Educational Supplement* one day, I found an advertisement for a violin teacher at a convent school in Salisbury. It was a threequarter-time post, but it was a start. I had an interview and got the job.

After that everything fell into place quite easily. My mother, who has been on her own since my father died fifteen years ago, lives in a Dorset village not far away, and she was pleased at my decision; she started sending me the local paper to help me find somewhere to live. Poppy and I made a list of possible properties for rent and we drove down together one day with Jess strapped into her seat in the back of Poppy's new Volvo.

Jerusalem Farm was almost impossible to find, tucked into a meandering valley away from anywhere. When we eventually did arrive, the agent for the estate, who had arranged a time to meet us, was standing looking furiously at his watch in the lane.

'So sorry,' said Poppy sweetly as we drew up, and the sight of her tangled mane of black hair and slanting eyes changed his manner almost instantly. I'm afraid I was probably a disappointment when I got out of the passenger door and shook his hand.

He couldn't take his eyes off Poppy in her cut-off shorts and endless legs.

She hitched Jess onto her hip and we set off to look at the cottage. It had a kitchen with a dirty cream Rayburn, a sitting room with an open fire and stairs to two bedrooms and a lovely little white bathroom. Its roof sat neatly over the upstairs windows and the contours of the land fitted snugly around it so it seemed to shrug its shoulders and nestle into the hill behind. I fell instantly in love.

'It's so lonely,' said Poppy. Then: 'Oh my God! What's that?'

'A cow,' said the delighted agent, laughing. 'It's a cow mooing.'

'What a bloody awful noise!' she shuddered.

'I love it,' I said, peering out of the bedroom window. 'May I?' indicating I'd like to open it and look out. The window was stiff but suddenly gave and I leaned out to look at the jumbled lawn and remnants of a flowerbed and the orchard beyond. As far as I could see were green fields neatly tucked and trimmed and threaded with woodland.

Poppy drew her cardigan round her shoulders and shivered. 'Is this place haunted?' she asked. 'Any hung highwaymen, pregnant milkmaids – that sort of thing?'

'Never heard of any here,' said the agent, smiling. 'It's all quite peaceful, as far as I know.'

I drew my head in from the window. 'If it is haunted,' I said, 'it's a good ghost. A kindly spirit. I can feel it in my bones.'

It was all settled then. The agent seemed to approve of the fact that I was a respectable teacher. The last tenants, I gathered, had been a bit New Age and Alternative, not much given to cleaning and repairs. He was pleased I had no children or pets and that the rent seemed reasonable to me. I forgot to ask about things like central heating or whether the lane was passable in the winter. Poppy thought I was mad and said so all the way back to London, which took two and a half hours. I knew I had done the right thing. I used Robert as a referee.

⊏══⊐

After that first afternoon alone with Robert I was left wondering if I had made a fool of myself and if I was ever going to hear from him again. I felt stupidly in love and wrote a poem to him on these lines, clumsy and poorly constructed but full of heartfelt meaning. I sent it off to his London office in a brown envelope marked PRIVATE. I enclosed no letter or note. A day later I had a telephone call in the middle of the morning when people with normal occupations would be at work. He was ringing from Heathrow on his way to Amsterdam. I could hear all the airport hubbub in the background.

'Sweetie,' he said. 'Sweetie, thank you so much. The poem was wonderful. I've written you one in return. Thinking of you all the time. See you soon,' and we were cut off.

I put the telephone down in a state of agitation. He was falling in love with me – I knew it. His cool manner had gone entirely. He had sounded breathless with emotion. I felt suddenly confident that I could win him. After all, I had youth and beauty and talent on my side. I had no intention of wrenching him away from his wife, but I did want a protestation of love. I wanted a conquest. I wanted him to sigh and suffer for me. I went over the brief conversation again and again. I could still recall the exact inflexion in his voice. What had I said in return? Very little. I hadn't had the chance. The sun was shining through the windows of my bedroom and making a warm square on my bed. I felt uplifted and full of excited happiness. He loved me.

The next morning I waited for the post and made myself extremely late for a rehearsal, then had to lie about a doctor's appointment. I seized the stiff cream envelope with unfamiliar black writing . . . lovely swooping artistic writing, ripped it open and hastily read the contents. It was a single sheet of matching, expensive card-like paper. The poem he'd written me was short and witty, perfectly rhymed and scanned. It spoke teasingly of middle-aged lust.

> Be assured I think of you a lot,
> My feelings range from warm to piping hot . . .

That sort of thing. I stuffed the envelope in my pocket and hurried out. I was pleased that he'd written for me, but disappointed by the lack of ardour. I read it again several times on the Tube and forced myself to feel amused at his style and self-deprecating wit. It was what I should have expected.

I was at this time going out in a rather half-hearted way with a man called Jeremy who worked in advertising. After Robert my feelings towards him changed. At twenty-seven, a bit younger than me, he suddenly seemed gauche and graceless. I was tired of his trendiness, his preoccupation with what was cool and fashionable. When he rang as he usually did to ask me if I was going to the pub on Saturday night, I said no. I wasn't anyway because I had a concert, but I also felt as if I wouldn't be seeing him again. We'd been to bed together, reasonably successfully if I'd drunk enough, but not very often because neither of us pursued one another with much conviction. We knew we weren't going anywhere and now seemed the time to break off. Jeremy wasn't heart-broken.

'Have you met someone?' he asked.

'No,' I lied.

I became obsessed with missing a telephone call. I dialled 1471 even if I'd only been out for five minutes to get a paper from the corner shop. I already had an answering service, essential to a performer, but there was never any message. I found out later that Robert never left one as a point of principle, distrusted the very idea of leaving a potentially incriminating message on a machine. I took out my diary and tried to work out the number of days he said he would be away. I couldn't remember. Eventually I telephoned his office number and the bitch secretary said he was abroad.

'Can you tell me when he will be back?' I asked.

'To whom am I speaking?' she enunciated.

I panicked and rang off, pulled myself together and rang back, said I'd dropped the telephone. I explained that I was a musician who had met Mr Mackintosh professionally. She unbent a little and explained that he was in Amsterdam for two more days, after which he would be only briefly in London before going straight back to his home in Scotland. However, she would tell him I had telephoned. She asked me what my business with him was, implying that she should know if it was something professional. I floundered and said, 'Oh, it's about a concert I'm giving,' and ended the conversation.

He had asked me not to tell Poppy about our relationship. He had all the caution of a married man and was wise enough to know that he had much more to lose than I did through indiscretion. He flattered me by saying that he knew instinctively that he could trust me, that I was an intelligent girl who understood his terms. I did indeed feel foolishly proud that he recognised me as an independent woman for whom a sexual affair with no strings attached was a possibility, an expression of a mutual need. I decided that I wouldn't tell Poppy the whole truth, only amuse her with details of our lunch. She knew too many people who knew him, and might well let something slip to her father. Musicians are terrible gossips.

So I kept the secret of my afternoon to myself, or almost. I did tell Loops, my cousin, eight years my junior, who knew no one in the music business – not classical anyway; pop stars and their ghastly managers sometimes took models from her agency to clubs, but that was it. Loops, always a good listener when not woken from a drug-induced sleep, thought it all very exciting.

'An older man,' she mused. 'Does that mean yachts and things?'

'No chance,' I laughed.

'Well, at least you've got rid of Jeremy.'

I went on a diet. I wrote SOLID in large letters and stuck it on the wall. I starved for two days and then had a huge Chinese blow-out with Loops who called round after a modelling assignment. She'd been standing in a bikini in dry ice all day and was chilled to the bone and famished. I put her in a hot bath and we ordered enough for four from the takeaway. I went to collect it from along the road and when I came back, Loops was drifting about in a bath towel, smoking.

'Your man rang,' she said. 'Or at least I assume it was him. He wouldn't leave his name. Very cagey.'

'Oh no!' I screamed. 'I can't bear it. What did he say? Did he leave a message?'

'He said he'd ring back. He's got a lovely voice – very deep and sexy. Are you sure he's not black?'

'Did he ask who you were?'

'No,' said Loops, stuffing batter-covered pork balls into her beautiful mouth. I regret to say that I did the same. Not into her mouth, of course, but mine.

He telephoned again, quite late that night. Loops had just left, taken away by her boyfriend on the back of his motorbike. I was lying on the sofa feeling uncomfortably full and regretting my over-indulgence as I always do, and wishing I could introduce a little moderation into my life.

'Hello,' he said in his gravelly voice.

24

'Hello,' I squeaked, shocked.

'How are YOU?' I don't know how he says it that way without it sounding corny, but he does.

'Fine.' I'd got control of my voice again. 'Pretty *solid*, actually.'

There was a pause. He didn't know what I was talking about. 'How was the trip?' I went on.

'Dull stuff, really. A meeting on copyrighting and a chance to check on a publishing house we have an interest in. Can I see you?'

'What, now?'

'Tomorrow. I'm fairly knackered now, so why don't we meet for breakfast?'

Thank God I had no rehearsals scheduled. 'Where?'

He named a hotel I'd never heard of, near the Embankment.

'Fine,' I said. We agreed a time and that was it.

'Until tomorrow. Goodnight, my lovely girl.' And he was gone.

<hr/>

Organising my move from London was not difficult. I surrendered the lease on my flat, glad that I hadn't been tempted into buying, and sorted out my bits of furniture to take down to Somerset. I decided to ask Loops and her current boyfriend, a Pakistani prince, or so he said, very handsome and affected, to help me and we hired a van and trundled off early one morning.

'Goodbye, Knightsbridge,' I sang as we crashed gears up the Brompton Road towards the M4, the M3, the A303 and the green green grass of my new home.

'You'll be back,' warned Loops darkly. She was wearing a beaten-up pair of leopard-skin cowboy boots and jeans so tight they looked a health hazard. When we stopped at Fleet services for breakfast and she loaded her plate with sausage, eggs, beans, bacon and fried bread, the whole restaurant came to a standstill. Men of whatever age stopped chewing and gazed in wonder while their wives glared disapprovingly.

So did the prince, come to that. He got in a mood and wouldn't speak. He didn't cheer up until we unpacked everything onto the long grass of the front lawn of Jerusalem Farm and there was no one to admire his girlfriend apart from him.

We hauled and shoved and heaved everything into place and nearly killed ourselves struggling to get my bed and a wardrobe up the stairs. At that point, the agent – Toby, as I was now invited to call him – arrived to ask if everything was all right. If Poppy had had an effect on him, it was as nothing to Loops. She had stripped off to a tiny singlet, her smooth brown stomach uncovered and her perfect breasts clearly outlined in their braless condition. The prince started to sulk again. We all sat on the grass and Loops smoked disgusting little roll-your-own cigarettes and I handed round beers I'd brought in a cool box.

'What do you think, Loops?' I asked as, lying back on an elbow, I surveyed the cottage.

'Bliss,' she said. 'I'll have to have a party here. You'll invite me for weekends, won't you? I can come down here to chill out with my mates.'

Toby looked anguished, clearly worried at the prospect and by the hostile glowering, tribal-looking young man sitting next to him, and yet thrilled at the same time.

'You don't need to be invited,' I said. 'What's mine is yours, baby.'

It started to rain and we had to scuttle about and cram in everything still on the lawn, any old how, before going to the pub in the village for a ploughman's lunch.

It rained incessantly after that, for four days at least. I had no telephone and no car, although Loops had promised to drive my old Renault down from London. Stupidly, I had forgotten the recharger for my mobile telephone. I felt cut off, lonely and utterly miserable.

The cottage reeked of damp, the flagstones downstairs glistened with wet and I failed dismally to light the Rayburn which meant I had no hot water except what I boiled in the kettle. Although I had lived on my own in London since I was twenty, there had always been the noises of other lives around me. I was used to hearing footsteps from the flat above, music playing from downstairs, muffled voices, doors closing, drunks on the street at night. Now silence enclosed me and it had a strange brooding quality. I could hear the hum of the fridge, the ticking of a clock, the creak of a floorboard. The cottage seemed to have a stilly life of its own. The quiet air in the rooms felt thick and swarming as I moved about putting things away, and in bed at night, the dark pressed down on me. I felt disconnected, afraid, watchful. The cottage was testing me, trying me out.

On the third day my mother came to visit me and I fell upon her with ill-concealed delight and relief. She had brought a basket which I unpacked onto the kitchen table – containing jam, honey, a scented candle, a home-made sponge cake and a bunch of flowers from her garden. She took off her coat and rolled up her sleeves and showed me how to light the bloody stove, twisting up paper and laying on twigs and small lumps of coal she'd found in the shed, and opening up a damper thing in the chimney.

'Why didn't that useless Toby show me all this?' I complained.

'Because I expect he thought you knew,' she said sweetly. 'Most people could have worked it out.'

'No, he was too busy swooning over Loops.'

In an hour or so the kitchen grew warm and with the flowers in a jug on the table and tea made, I felt cheered up.

'I'll take you into the village where you can telephone British Telecom and Laura' (Loops's proper name) 'and buy some provisions at the shop. You're going to need to order some more coke soon for that stove, too.' My mother was taking over my life again and for the moment I was terribly grateful. I remembered how she looked after us as children when we had flu, smoothing pillows and preparing hot lemon drinks and making us feel better just by being competently in charge.

'You are a dear old thing,' I said fondly, touching her hand.

'Enough of the old,' she replied tartly. Then: 'Well, this is charming, or at least it will be,' she said a moment later as she looked out of the kitchen window where the sun had begun to shine weakly. The hot-water tap was now running encouragingly warm as I washed up. 'You must make the stove up again before you go out,' she ordered. 'Fill up the hod in the coal shed and keep it by the door.'

'Hod,' I said, lingering over the word. 'I can't believe I'm the owner of a *hod*.'

'Keeper, more like,' said my ma dryly. 'It came with the cottage. It's not yours.'

'Yes, Ma.'

There was no one about in the village, but I bought a few things at the shop – tinned sardines, baked beans, white bread, bacon, eggs (factory farmed as far as I could tell – so much for the country life), and told the lady at the till that I was the new tenant at Jerusalem Farm. I expected her to react with interest, as would have been the case in *The Archers*.

'Oh yes?' she said. End of conversation.

I went to the telephone which was in a proper red box on the Green and arranged with BT to call at the end of the week to hitch me up or whatever you do with phone lines; I also left a message on Loops's answermachine that I was getting desperate for my car. I tried to contact Poppy but she was out. Her new Danish au pair answered and said that she was at the

28

doctor's: she was expecting her second baby. I sent love and said that I'd let her have my new number as soon as I got it. Finally, I telephoned Robert, with my mother sitting patiently in her shiny little car, and got his answerphone. I rang off, thought about what to say and then rang back and left a brief message.

'Hi. It's me. Been pretty bloody so far. Better now. Sun's come out. I should have a telephone by the end of the week so I'll get in touch then. Bye.'

I tried to imagine his answermachine whirring, storing my message in his office in his home in the Borders. I pictured an oak-lined room, an imposing desk, long windows overlooking the sweeping gardens and the distant figure of Mary bossing some Scottish gardener around. As I came out of the telephone box, I had a sudden brainwave and dived back into the shop. My eyes had not deceived me, it was indeed licensed to sell alcohol. I bought a large bottle of whisky. Things were going to be all right.

'For my mother,' I lied to the assistant, who managed to look disapproving while she wrapped the bottle in paper. She looked doubtfully through the window at where my mother sat in her Fiesta listening to *Gardeners' Question Time*.

Chapter Four

Going off to have breakfast with Robert that first time was not as easy as it may sound. First of all I had a sleepless night beforehand and lay awake worrying that I'd look tired as well as 'solid' and that I had nothing suitable to wear. As relationships mature one tends to forget the electric charge of those early meetings: the nervous anticipation; the almost sickening expectation of being with someone who has been allowed to monopolise one's thoughts.

I intended to get up early and wash my hair, but in the end it was dawn before I fell asleep and then I overslept. I hurtled about with wet hair trying to decide how I should look and ended up in a long linen skirt and a plain shirt – understated but chic, I thought. Trousers were out of the question after I'd eaten so much the night before. At least my blonde hair was shiny and hung in a floating curtain when I hastily blew it dry. What a great asset it is to be blonde, I thought, not knowing then that he actually prefers redheads. Like Helen.

I took a taxi and when I went into the hotel found that there were two dining rooms, one called the Thames Terrace and the other the Trafalgar. I opted for the Thames Terrace and saw him straight away, reading a newspaper with his back to me but facing a large wall mirror, so that if he cared to look up, he could see anyone entering the room.

I had forgotten how big, how substantial he was. He looked sleek and beautifully dressed. He wore a silk tie, and a matching handkerchief peeked out from his breast pocket. His shirt was immaculate and his cuff-links chunky gold and expensive-looking. His charcoal suit wasn't creased or rumpled and as he stood to kiss me he shook each leg of his trousers down to cover his shiny shoes. He was freshly shaved and smelled pleasantly of some citrus fruit. I thought disparagingly of Jeremy and his ugly and tasteless leisure clothes in pastel colours, and the shiny Italian suits he wore to work.

Robert kissed me on the mouth and in the mirror I saw other breakfasters – nearly all men – take notice.

'Come and eat,' he said. 'I expect you're starving. I certainly am.' The hotel ran a kind of breakfast buffet with everything you could imagine, hot and cold. I took yoghurt and fruit and he did the same. I'd have loved bacon and eggs. Have you noticed how when you really overeat you are twice as hungry the next morning? Anyway, I didn't like to display my healthy appetite again. He, on the other hand, had no such inhibitions and went along the line of hot dishes, piling his plate.

We sat down and coffee, strong and hot, was brought by a foreign girl. In fact, all the waiters and waitresses were non-English speakers, so much so that when he asked for a spoon it threw the entire catering department into confusion and there were worried exchanges in something that sounded like Portuguese. After a long wait, he went to look for one himself. You would have thought someone would have taught the staff 'knife, spoon, fork, plate'. It had rained earlier but was now a splashily bright London morning and a brisk wind blew high clouds across the bit of sky I could see out of the plate-glass windows. It seemed odd to be having breakfast with someone when I hadn't spent the night with them. It was like starting

32

from cold, or beginning where one might normally expect to finish.

'Well, how have you been?'

'Missing you.' Oh God! Why was I so shameless?

'Aah,' he said, 'sweet thing,' and he made a kissing shape with his mouth. He has healthy red lips, full and well-shaped, but never wet. It is the sort of mouth designed for sensual pleasures. The opposite of 'thin-lipped'.

I hastened on with a funny account of rehearsals and a concert I'd played in, and he laughed and was very relaxed and happy. He told me about some difficulty in Amsterdam that he was supposed to have sorted out, and how it had been a tiring and frustrating visit. The waiter kept filling up our coffee cups. Eventually he looked at his watch. It was 10.15.

'What are your plans?' he asked.

'I don't have any immediate plans,' I said.

'I have to catch a plane from Stansted at two this afternoon, so I don't have all that long. I must go and collect my suitcase from the Club, but that's only around the corner. Will you come with me?'

'Of course,' I said happily. I'd go anywhere he wanted.

He paid the bill and I knew the waiters were looking at me as we left, hand in hand. We were so obviously not married. Me, twenty-seven and he in his fifties. He holds hands really well – never too hot or clammy or sticky, but dry and firm. It is like being led along. Sometimes he tucks my hand into his arm, and that's lovely too. We reached his club and he went in first, telling me to walk to the end of the street and back before joining him on the second floor in his room. I walked carefully and unhurriedly. I remembered reading somewhere that Marilyn Monroe walked putting one foot exactly in front of the other. It was this that gave her that unmistakable wiggle. I experimented with this and found it quite hard to do. I enjoyed the feeling that I was playing the part of the forbidden fruit. It made me feel especially chosen, choice, desirable.

'Good morning, madam,' said the porter as I went in.

'Good morning,' I replied and wiggled past to the lift, head high. I was getting used to being a mistress.

We made love of course, and it was wonderful, better than the first time even, although I realised that he had an eye on his bedside clock. Then he bustled about packing. He is one of those men who have cases for everything, with special compartments. He must have a lot of rich relations who rack their brains for ideas for Christmas presents. His silver brush went into a perfect little leather case, his shoe-cleaning kit into another.

I lay lazily on the bed watching him.

'I've brought you a little present from Amsterdam,' he said lovingly, rummaging in a bag. I sat up. Amsterdam! Precious stones – little sparkly diamonds to mark the beginning of a wonderful affair? He gave me a round object, larger than a cricket ball, wrapped in creased paper. I unwrapped it carefully. It was an Edam cheese. I could have thrown it through the bloody window.

It was late July when I moved out of London and I had almost five weeks before my teaching started. Concert performances had dried up, and although I had a few days' work booked in my diary, I was more or less free of obligations. Money was tight and there were things I would have liked to do in the cottage which would have to wait.

By the time Loops delivered my car, after driving round the district for hours getting herself more and more lost, I'd discovered that bus services in the country are virtually non-existent. I met several milk tankers on my walks to the village and had to leap into the hedges to let them past. A milk-tanker taxi service would be a good idea, but most of the drivers weren't friendlylooking and I suppose one would end up calling at every dairy farm in the area rather than going where most people would want to go, like the Post Office or the mobile library. The woman at the shop was no more talkative. I realised that she'd written me off as a week-ender – someone who was preventing her Andy and Shuna from being able to afford to live in their own village. She had discussed this issue loudly in front of me several times.

I looked into the church one afternoon and sat for a while in its cool interior. I'd forgotten what churches smell like – old hymn books and dusty carpets overlaid with polish and stagnant water from the flower arrangements. I thought about that lovely Philip Larkin poem and how well it summed up how I felt – uninvolved and yet part of it all, and glad that it still stood, squat grey and reassuring. I looked at the flower rota and the Sunday School rota, and the Sea Breezes Club and a notice about a trip to Swanage. It seemed as if this parish was looked after by a rector who had four other churches as well, and that there were only services here once a month.

At this moment a female vicar opened the door and came in. She looked surprised to see me, just sitting there, and as if she hoped I wasn't going to turn out to be someone in trouble. I gave her a cheerful smile and she perked up. She was small and round with a grey bob and owly glasses. Although she had on ordinary clothes, she also wore a dog collar and bib thing inside her jacket. It looked a funny and uncomfortable arrangement, like women wearing ties. She asked me if I was a visitor – this village, apart from being pretty, is not distinguished by anything to bring tourists to it – and I said no, I'd just moved into Jerusalem Farm. She looked interested then and I could see her wondering if I'd got kiddies for her

Sunday School because she said, 'Have you got a family?'

'No. Single,' I said, in a bright tone so that she could see I didn't mind. She said she'd make sure that I'd get the parish magazine delivered and made me fill in a form for new parishioners.

When Loops brought my car I was finally able to recharge my mobile phone (I'd left the gadgetry for this on the back seat), and started to feel much less cut off. Loops was wonderfully enthusiastic and we went off into the nearest town, found a Waitrose and bought delicious and exotic things for our supper. Loops scooted and hung on the trolley and behaved like a child and people stared as usual. Although she was wearing old jeans and a grubby T-shirt she still looked beautiful beyond belief.

The fat girl with brittle blonde hair working the till gazed at her with unconcealed admiration mixed with despair. 'I know the feeling,' I felt like saying. 'She makes me feel just the same.' Beauty in such abundance has made Loops careless with people, I noticed. She doesn't bother to thank ordinary people enough for small services. She doesn't look at them or smile. 'Hey,' I said when we were in the car, 'you completely ignored that girl on the till.'

Loops looked at me oddly. 'What do you mean?'

'Well, you know, you didn't thank her, or say goodbye.'

'For God's sake. She was doing her bloody job, and bloody slowly, too. Why should I thank her?'

I didn't answer.

Robert was away most of that July. I can't quite remember where, but walking in Italy was part of it. This was the only sort of holiday Mary would tolerate. I could imagine her striding ahead of him up a mountain, while he puffed behind hoping it was nearly lunchtime. After that he had a trip to the States and a few days fishing in

Ireland. He sent me entertaining and witty postcards. I propped them behind the teapot in my new kitchen and looked at them from time to time. I also thought a lot about him visiting me down here in the country. I have to admit that the choice of this cottage was heavily influenced by a fantasy I had of him staying with me for a while. In fact, he promised he would. He had never come to my flat in London, but obviously felt that the country was more discreet. Nearly everything I did, as I explored the fields and lanes, made me think of doing the same thing, but with him.

My picture of Mary wasn't drawn entirely from imagination, or by piecing together what Robert had told me. Of course I'd never seen her in the flesh, but he'd shown me a photograph. On about our third meeting he'd told me to bring photographs to the next, to help fill in the gaps in our lives. I'd agonised over the choice, but found some pretty ones of me as a child with my sister and brother, and some of where we'd grown up in Barnes. I felt sad looking at one of my father, David. He had been a Classics master at St Paul's and died when I was eighteen. I decided not to take it with me. It seemed inappropriate somehow.

Robert came with a whole album and we sat up in bed drinking wine out of tooth glasses and he showed them to me. His house in Scotland was massive. 'It's Mary's,' he explained. 'She inherited it from her uncle.' It wasn't beautiful but made a terrific statement about the importance of its owners – being a show-off sort of Victorian schloss with turrets and gothic windows.

'God!' I said. I decided not to show him our semi-detached house in Barnes. It wasn't that I was ashamed, I just didn't want to have it diminished by contrast. I'd loved it there, growing up in a noisy, talented family with my calm, dreamy father, ignorant then of his defective heart, and my busy, practical, homemaking mother.

'Here,' he said, indicating with his finger, 'is where Mary wants a lake.'

'Mary wants a lake?' I had to think about this. Would I want a lake? I didn't think so, and couldn't imagine how you'd know, for sure, that that was what you wanted. Awful to dig it, and then find out you didn't.

'Here she is,' he said of the next photograph. I began to feel uneasy. Is it all right to lie in bed with your mistress and show her photographs of your wife? However, I studied it with interest. Mary was in her early fifties. She had orangey-coloured hair held back by a hairband, and was tall and slim. She was wearing one of those pie-necked frill blouses favoured by women with loud upper-class voices, and an M&S cardigan which I recognised because my mother has one, and a pair of jeans, ironed – I could see the crease. She was smiling and seemed rather pleasant. She had a determined-looking chin.

'She looks nice. Is she pretty?'

'Not pretty, but attractive. Well-preserved. Fit – much fitter than me. You can see she's tall and thin. She used to be a model at one time.'

Okay, I thought. I hate you, Mary. I was annoyed by the way he described her. Affectionately. Admiringly.

'Not solid, then?' I said.

'What?' Not understanding.

'Well, why don't you love her?' I changed the question.

'Too difficult to answer, my love. She's not an easy or a happy person. She's basically discontented, dissatisfied . . . she thinks people always let her down.' Perhaps she's right, I thought. 'A very unhappy childhood, father away all the time in the Army, a bitch of a mother . . . a pretty hopeless sort of education. Marriage was all she was prepared for, and she couldn't wait to get away from home. I came along and that was it.'

'Why did you marry her? Did you love her then?'

'I thought I did. I really fancied her. A lot of men did. I still do.'

What the hell are you doing here? I thought.

'What the hell are you doing here?' I asked.

'She doesn't want to have sex. After the children, she said she had retired. We have separate rooms. She sees a specialist about a back problem. Now stop asking questions and make love to me.'

So I did, but there was something about what he'd said that spoiled the afternoon. Already there was a gathering of forces which seemed to threaten the small space I felt I occupied in his life.

<hr>

After I put Loops on the train back to London and waved her goodbye, I drove slowly back to the farm through the jungly lanes grown high with all sorts of rampant green things, which I couldn't identify then, but can now. I stopped in a gateway and picked some wild honeysuckle and watched some pheasants strutting about a field. They were bright and gaudy-looking birds with silly expressions. The farmers were combining busily while the good weather lasted, and as I drove I kept meeting tractors hurtling along with trailers full of grain.

By the time I turned onto my farm track I knew that what I needed was not a lake, but a dog. I scrabbled about in my pile of newspapers, set aside for recycling, and found last week's local paper which had a page entitled *Pets and Livestock*. It's a funny word, livestock. It sounds as if there ought to be Deadstock advertised somewhere, and for all I know there is. The whole of the country seems to be dedicated to killing things – shooting pheasants, or hunting foxes, driving lambs and sheep and cows to be slaughtered. I was determined, however, not to be a townie about this. Also, I love eating meat.

Eventually I found the page I'd been looking for and

ran my eyes down it. An advertisement put in by the local pet rescue home caught my attention straight away: *Gentle rescued greyhound seeking quiet country home. No cats.*

I telephoned the number and spoke to a woman who said the dog in question was called Pilgrim's Progress; he was four years old, a not very successful racing dog who had been neglected. She asked me a lot of questions and seemed pleased with my answers. It was rather like computer dating and I felt excited as she fixed up our first meeting.

The next day I went to see him and he was really disappointing in the flesh. It was as if a short fat man of fifty-five, whose main interest is tropical fish, had described himself as tall, dark, fascinating, young and handsome. Poor Pilgrim, who I had imagined as lean and graceful, was skin and bone with patches on his sides denuded of hair.

'Mange,' said the rescue lady, 'and he has been half-starved as you can see, and tied up here.' She showed me a ring of raw flesh round his neck. 'He needs a great deal of love and attention. That's why we were looking for a single person, rather than a family. He's not fit for family life yet.' Like me, I thought.

I have to confess I thought he looked perfectly hideous, but he gazed up at me with eyes of such liquid beauty that I had no choice. The lady gave me a list of things I should buy, treatments for mange and the sort of diet he needed, and told me he had been wormed. He jumped eagerly into the back of my car and rested his long nose on his paws. I stopped in a little town and found a pet shop and bought all the things on the list, including a proper greyhound collar and leash and a great squashy dog bed. When I lugged it back to the car he was standing in the front seat looking desperate and shaking. He was so pleased to see me. It brought tears to my eyes and I drove home sniffing and promising him out loud that I would never leave him or forsake him. Never.

Of course, I did. The moment Robert wanted me in London I packed Pilgrim up and sent him to my mother.

Chapter Five

It is not difficult to remember exactly when I found out about Helen. After that breakfast meeting I came away with more than the Edam. While Robert was in the bathroom I had snatched up his Filofax which he had left on the bedside table and although I knew I shouldn't be rifling through it, I took a glimpse inside the cover which furnished me with his home address and telephone number, also an office number he used for business calls and faxes at his home in Scotland. I scribbled them down on a scrap of paper and shoved it in my bag.

I don't know exactly why this subterfuge seemed necessary, but I had already realised that he kept back far more than he gave away and it seemed that I was not allowed more than a chink of a view of his other armour-plated life. There was a massive inequality in this state of affairs. I had nothing to hide from him. My life was simple, open, threadbare even, and I was happy for him to share any of it. Our relationship was becoming a major part of my existence, whereas I, for him, occupied only the suburbs of his life. The main thrust of his energy was directed elsewhere. Later on I even started to invent complications, lunch dates, new friends, dinner parties to make things seem a little less lopsided and to give my life more dimension, to make it seem fuller, less pitiful.

The next day I decided to make use of the information and to telephone him at home. I wanted to intrude on his other life, to invade it in some way with a reminder of me. I dialled his office number. He answered almost on the first ring.

'Hello,' I said in my sexiest voice.

'Helen? Hello, darling.'

'No. It's not Helen. It's me.'

There was only a moment's pause. 'Harriet? Hello. How nice to hear from you.' He didn't ask me how I knew his number.

'Who's Helen?'

A pause. Then: 'A friend. Why?'

'I just wondered who Helen Darling was?'

'Now don't be silly.'

'Well, tell me who she is.' My voice appalled me, whining, full of hostility.

'A friend.'

'Hmmm.'

'What is that supposed to mean?'

'Whatever you like.'

This ridiculous conversation was not going anywhere but I didn't seem able to stop it. Robert did.

'Look, I'll call you back this evening. There's not much point in continuing like this.'

'Okay.' I felt furious – with him and with me. He was so bloody cool and unruffled and I had behaved like a petulant child. What right had I to demand to know who this Helen was? Why should I be told? Actually, I knew exactly why. Because I suspected he had another lover who was allowed to telephone him at home. The more I thought about it, the more convinced I became.

I spent the rest of the day nervous and restless. I had a rehearsal to go to which dragged on and I found the conductor irritating and his many interruptions fussy and pedantic. I played carelessly and longed to be free to go back home where I could think on my own. In the end I went to have a drink with some of the other players and forced myself to be cheerful and lively. I did not want to sit in my flat waiting for his call.

By the time he telephoned me back, and I knew he would because he is, if nothing else, a man of his word, I had worked out how I felt. I most certainly wanted exclusive rights to him. I knew I had to share him with Mary, but her claim on him was quite different from mine. I could accept the two of them as official fellow travellers, first-class of course, shackled together by marriage and children. What was more, he had said to me that he didn't love Mary and that they didn't make love. But I couldn't stand the idea of another lover. This was direct competition and I wasn't prepared to share.

He might describe our affair as a 'lustful friendship' and declare that he was reconciled to the fact that I was quite likely to have other more convenient and available lovers, but he knew I didn't and that I was unlikely to. The very business of sleeping with him made that, for me, impossible. However much I might have been brain-washed into believing that sex could be guilt-free and no-strings attached, for me it could never be like that. Surely only the very promiscuous can sleep with people and remain untouched? Ordinary men and women are too full of human frailties, too anxious, too vulnerable. I knew I couldn't like naked in his arms without believing that this was important to him, that I was the person he most wanted. Only then could I give myself to him in the abandoned way of lovers.

Casual sex had never been a possibility for me. Even with Jeremy we'd both been trying to make each other significant and hoped that sex might help. The will was there even if the flesh wasn't up to it. Oh dear, this wasn't turning out as I had planned. Embarking on an affair with a married man considerably older than me had seemed like an exciting adventure. I was prepared to be spoiled and adored. I was prepared to abide by his rules and not upset his other life and to accept that he didn't believe in love. I thought that I could prove him wrong. Now the goal posts had been moved mid-game.

He telephoned at 9.30 p.m. He sounded cheerful and relaxed and not cross or nervous. We chatted for a bit and I managed to match his mood. It was he who changed the subject and said, 'Now – about Helen. Do you want me to tell you the truth, even though it will hurt and annoy you, or do you want to let the whole thing drop and we can, if you wish, go on as before?'

'You must tell me,' I said at once. As if there was really a choice. He told me briefly that Helen was a woman whom he had known when they were growing up. She was a teenage love. At nineteen he had been totally infatuated by her. She was then amazingly attractive and popular and had hardly noticed him. Later she moved away, went to university and they saw one another rarely. Both married, Helen to a clever Jew, a lawyer. Helen's marriage was brilliant and admired. Her husband was very successful and became wealthy and they lived in a series of increasingly expensive and beautiful houses in London. They had two children, equally clever and bright. The third was born with Down's syndrome. Helen's husband made her put the little boy into a private home. From then on their marriage fell apart. Helen doted on the damaged Ben. Her husband, resentful, took a series of mistresses. At fifteen, last year, Ben died and Helen left her husband, or rather, asked him to leave her. It was at this point that Robert came back into her life.

'How did you meet again?' I asked. 'I thought you said you'd lost contact all those years ago.'

'Helen found me. It wasn't really very difficult, as she knew I worked in the family business. She rang me at the office and asked me out to dinner. Mary by that time had moved up to Scotland, although we still had the flat in London. I felt a bit neglected and was lonely and so I went. I was also extremely curious to see her again. Helen's daughter, Belinda, was there to lend an air of respectability. She only stayed for dinner and left early to go to a club or something with a boyfriend. I knew that Helen was giving me encouraging signals. She asked a lot of leading questions . . . gave me too much to drink. Later she confessed that she had made up her mind that if she still found me attractive she would seduce me. She was lonely, too, and a newly separated woman of fifty can find it difficult to meet men, as friends as well as lovers.'

Oh, I knew the Helen type, I thought furiously. I could imagine her casting off the husband who had given her a comfortable but painful life, and looking through her address book for the next. She would seek a man who could reassure her that she was still beautiful and desirable. A rich, confident man of her own class with whom she could continue to lead a glossy and privileged life. She chose the man who had once worshipped her, and intended to revive those feelings of heady youth in them both. I suppose her motives weren't that much worse than mine, but I found mine easier to live with. I simply wanted a lover. I suspected that Helen wanted more.

'Is she still beautiful?' I asked.

'Well, she's in her early fifties, but yes, she is a very attractive woman.'

I tried to think of someone this old who was still attractive. In fact, I couldn't think of anyone I even knew well who was that old. I felt angry and sick. I thought of tortoise necks and the stringy brown arms and collapsed armpits of wealthy older women who take expensive holidays.

'So what happened?' I said dully.

'When I was saying goodbye I squeezed her bum and she responded passionately. That was the beginning.'

'Okay. So where do I fit into this touching drama?'

'You? Why, what have you to do with it?'

I didn't know how to respond to this, except by exploding, so I kept quiet.

Robert went on: 'Do you mean, does this make any difference to us? As far as I'm concerned, not in the slightest. But I do see that you might feel differently.'

'Yes, I do,' I said coldly. 'Does Helen know about me?'

'No, of course not.'

'Why of course not? I thought you prided yourself on your honesty.'

'There is no point in one's honesty causing hurt. I did offer not to tell you, but you insisted and I judged you deserved the truth. After all, Harriet, you are years younger than me, very attractive and must have men lusting after you by the dozen. I feel hugely flattered that you want me, but I don't for a moment believe that our affair is anything more than a question of satisfying a mutual need and could at any moment be brought to a close. Helen is much more vulnerable and is very damaged by the terrible grief she has suffered. I am her support at the moment and I would be wrong to hurt her. Actually she would be furious and chuck me out, I suspect, if she knew about you. She has, after all, had a very hard life. She has suffered terribly. Her husband is a cruel man. I couldn't inflict further unkindness on her.'

'Oh yes, poor Helen. How come she feels it's all right to recycle other people's husbands? Does she know Mary Mary Quite Contrary, oblivious in her garden?'

'No, they have never met. I can't answer your first question, but to be fair she might well ask it of you.'

'What is the sex like?' I had a vision of tough old skin and dug-like breasts.

'Since you ask such an inappropriate question, wonderful.'

At this point I had to laugh. Robert did too, quite heartily. I don't know why I laughed but it seemed that if I did, and convincingly, I was somehow proving that I was not hurt or foolish or deluded.

'Well?' he asked, eventually.

'Well what?'

'Oh do stop it. What do you want to do?' he asked. 'God, modern women. You are a nightmare!'

'What do I want to do? What do I want you to do, you mean?'

'No. That isn't what I asked. I'm not prepared to do anything.'

'Oh well, fuck off then. Anyway, you lied to me. You told me I was your only London screw.'

'How delightfully you put it. Helen lives most of the time now at her house in Suffolk and so I wasn't lying.'

He always manages to make me feel cheap and wrong, as if it is me who is behaving badly. But I knew it was his fault. He wasn't behaving as I imagined he should. He had departed from the script I had written for him.

This change in the nature of our affair took some getting used to. I spent a long time thinking about what Robert had told me and trying to work out how I felt. I didn't want to be defeated and to let him go. He fascinated me and without doubt had enhanced my life since he came into it. On the one hand I fought to keep my relationship with him light-hearted. He had left me with no delusions about how he felt about me and I was terrified of getting in too deep myself. However, Helen spoiled things. To be second string is a humiliating and diminishing experience. I had entered this affair to boost my confidence and self-esteem and to enjoy the heady pleasure of loving and being loved. My lover's preference for a woman nearly twice my age did not do me any favours. He made no attempt to hide the fact that he was enamoured by her. Once he asked me to stroll around outside his club for ten minutes while he called her on the telephone to make some arrangement to see her. I find it hard to believe that I complied. But I did.

The obvious thing to do was to end our affair at once. I nearly did this several times, by telephone, but thought I would wait until I saw him again. We had a date booked several weeks ahead when he was taking me out to dinner. Meanwhile he wrote to me often and his letters brought me a great deal of pleasure. They also confused me. To bother to sit and cover several pages in his beautiful handwriting, describing his life, his garden, his observations about what was in the news, suggesting books to read and music to listen to, seemed like the greatest compliment he could pay me. He said on the telephone that he felt freer to talk to me than anyone he'd known.

'What about Helen?' I heard myself asking as quick as a shot. It was me who brought Helen into everything. I couldn't help it and it made me wince. He remained remarkably good-natured.

'Helen? No. With Helen I mostly listen and give her support. I don't tell her much about me.' Selfish bitch, I thought.

I was lulled into partly accepting this strange and unsatisfactory state. I continued to see other friends, went to parties, even kissed other men, but Robert was there all the time in the background.

He took to telephoning me nearly every night at 11.30 p.m. He was a night owl and was always at his desk at that time. Mary, the early riser, was long since in her bed. Quite often he woke me up and I loved our drowsy conversations ending with him whispering, 'Sleep well, my darling. I wish I was there with you.' I was always left wondering how he could be like this with me and still want Helen.

One night I asked him when he rang her. A man of habit, he was sure to have a time. 'Nine-thirty, every morning,' he said honestly. 'Even if she's had children at home they've usually gone by then.'

After that I tried his number at 9.30 a.m. and sure enough, it was always engaged. I tried again and again and found he usually talked for half an hour. What a telephone bill he must have, I thought.

At the same time my jealousy increased. It began like a pea to germinate and sent out a green shoot which grew larger and larger. This bloody, bloody Helen, I thought. I hated everything about her. By asking the right questions I was able to form an impression of my rival. I thought of her like that although he insisted that she wasn't.

'You are completely and utterly different. Why should you be rivals?'

'Well, of course we are – for your affection at least!'

'Why? I'm inordinately fond of you both . . . in different ways. Why does it have to be a competition? I consider myself a very lucky man. Now come here and let me make love to you, you glorious girl.'

I sulked and pouted. I hated Helen for spoiling it.

'Do you tell her you love her?' I demanded.

'No. I've told you I don't go in for that. Helen understands that I will never leave Mary. She accepts that.'

Like hell! I thought.

'How do you know? Why doesn't she want more from you? She could, couldn't she? I mean, she could re-marry, couldn't she?'

'For the moment she is reasonably content with how things are. I have told her that she must not let me stand in her way of meeting other men. She is a woman who needs a man. Marriage suited her very well, even her unhappy one. She calls herself a serial monogamist.'

'Why can't she know about me?'

'Because at the moment there is no need. It would cause her grief and she isn't like you. She couldn't take it and I think would probably chuck me out. Selfishly, I don't want that.'

'Why do you think I can take it?'

'You are young, my dear. Life is still full of opportunities and you have a different outlook to people of our age. You are still open to new experiences and you damage so easily. You could bin me at the least notice, like you did poor Jeremy. I don't think it hurts you not having the opportunity to monopolise my feelings, for what they are worth. It might annoy you, but I don't think it hurts you. Anyway you can discard me if you don't like it.'

'I could tell Helen,' I said darkly.

Robert did not alter his tone one degree. 'I don't think you'll do that,' he said.

'Why not? How do you know?'

'Because you are intelligent and understand the consequences of such a thing.'

However I did think about it. I had no idea what Helen's surname was and Robert was not going to tell me. I did ask him but he smiled and said, 'Don't treat me as a fool.'

That was a problem. I had no address for her, or telephone number. I was stumped. In actual fact he was right, I could not have brought myself to the point of telling her the truth about her faithless lover anyway. What would it gain? The fact that I knew of her and she didn't know of me was comforting and made me feel powerful. I liked to think of her smug and self-satisfied in the beautiful house her husband had bought her, pleased with her conquest of Robert and unconscious of the worm in the apple she had helped herself to.

You'll pay for it, I told her. I don't know how, but you will.

Chapter Six

Poppy drove down to see me after I had been at Jerusalem Farm about three weeks. She was four months' pregnant and had the dearest little pod of a tummy to show for it. It made her cross because with Jess she hardly showed at all and never bought a single maternity marquee. Today she wore a pair of ordinary jeans but showed me how she couldn't do them up. She seemed happier and more contented these days. I told her so and she said, 'Yeah, like a cow.'

Things were better between her and Chris, who was proving to be what I always suspected, good husband material. He was loving and thoughtful and adored Poppy and Jess. The fact that he was about as interesting as ditchwater had not proved to be such a disadvantage. I had had the opportunity to look in ditches lately and they didn't seem that bad to me. A whole lot of irisy-type flowers grew in one near the cottage and it was always full of bustling and plopping noises as if there was a lot of activity going on in there.

Part of the wonder of Poppy's life was Jess, a sunny, happy child who instantly fell in love with Pilgrim, who also seemed to like her. She trotted round the garden towing him about with her hand on his collar, making him swerve on his spindly legs.

'What a perfectly frightful dog,' said Poppy. 'Why didn't you get what they call a working dog, one that picks things up or helps in the garden?'

Jess held my hand as we walked round the little patch I'd cleared. I showed her the old mower that I had found in an outhouse. I had had a go with it but gave up after it had pulled tangled loops of grass out of the would-be lawn and then become impossible to push, its blades utterly wodged with wet grass. I told her that Toby had said he would bring me some sheep to eat it all – some dear little brown and white Jacob sheep like I remembered in pictures of the Holy Land in my first Bible.

I took her to the place where I thought we could get someone like her daddy to put up a swing in the apple tree. Poppy and I agreed that we were hopeless examples of emancipated womanhood. Neither of us could begin to work out how you made a swing, and the washing line I had attempted to hang from the cottage wall to a tree had fallen down almost immediately – but not, of course, before I'd hung the washing on it. The nail I'd driven into the crumbly bits between the bricks had fallen straight out of the wall.

'Oh God, you need some special nail or drill – can't remember which,' Poppy said. 'You'll have to get a man with that sort of attachment. For heaven's sake don't get all *Good Life*-y, will you? I couldn't bear it if you had pockets full of slug pellets and a hairy chin. Drift about in a lace dress and make spiked lemonade, and you're sure to lure a passing man to help with all the boys' jobs.'

Some hope, I thought.

Jess was now nearly four and utterly enchanting. She had a mop of brown silky hair, wide brown eyes, peach-coloured skin and a tractable nature. I loved her to distraction. I showed her all the little nooks and crannies of the farm, the old pig pen and the shed where Toby said they used to keep a bull. These days, apparently, semen comes through the post and all the little calves in the fields are test tube babies. Some potatoes had appeared miraculously in the garden, remnants of those planted in the past by some gnarled old farmer. I showed them to Poppy.

'You are going completely barmy,' she said. 'Let's go to the pub.'

Later, while we sat outside in the Beer Garden and Jess chased the pub bantams trying to make them eat crisps, Poppy said, 'So has Robert been to see you?'

'Nope.'

'How does this withdrawal to the country affect things? Isn't it going to be even harder to see him now – or is that the whole point? Are you surrendering to Helen?'

I had given into temptation and told her about the other woman, the thorn in my side. 'Half and half. I don't think it makes it that much harder. I can be in London in just over two hours; he can come here where nobody knows him. I hope he will. I also think that it's time I try to make a different sort of life, Pops. I couldn't go on as I was. I'm the same age as you and yet compare us. You have a husband, one and a half children, a house, a mortgage, a Volvo, for God's sake, a nanny or whatever you call Jess's keeper, and so on. I've got a vanload of rubbish and an overdraft. This is my first conscious step towards settling down to something. This new job is permanent and will provide me with a steady income for the first time in my life. I can live quite cheaply here – there's nothing to spend money on as you will have observed – and I can try and make some sense of things. If I'm destined to be an old maid I'd rather be one down here, than go on racketing around in London, waking up with hangovers and living in pubs at weekends. It always seemed that I was waiting for my life to begin, as if I was hanging on because there was something just around the corner. Now I've stopped thinking that. I'm going to take control.'

'You'll never meet anyone here though, will you? The place seems utterly desolate – you hardly see a soul. What do all the people do who live in these grand houses scattered about? Are they all out slaughtering things all the time when they're not shopping in Waitrose, wearing jodhpurs?'

'The bar was full of men, didn't you notice?'

Poppy looked at me in a disconcerted way. 'Hatty! An old codger mumbling into his scrumpy and some pot-bellied yobboes in vests and tattoos, playing darts. Anyway, how long are you going to put up with this Helen nonsense?'

Our conversations often took this turn. I fiddled about with the stem of my glass, not wanting to look Poppy in the eye.

'It doesn't seem nonsense when I talk about it with him. He makes it sound utterly reasonable. Anyway, I don't have much choice but to like it or lump it.'

'But you've just been saying you are taking control, so you do have a choice. It's so bad for you. Being a mistress is miserable enough, I imagine – all those weekends and holidays when he's with his wife in the bosom of his family – but to have a time-share with this woman Helen. God! You really must love him to put up with it. The trouble is that you are not giving yourself a chance to make a new life here if you are going to hang onto him. I mean, what's in it for you? Where are the fur coats and the diamonds and the matching luggage and the little trips to Paris? They are only payment in kind, you know – the things that make all the suffering involved in being a mistress worthwhile. Don't men like him keep their mistresses in flats in London? He should be paying your rent, at least.'

I thought of the Edam and had to smile.

'It's never been like that,' I said. 'I wouldn't want it to be. Why should I be a kept woman? I'm not his, any more than he's mine.'

56

'Oh yes! Brave independent words. But while you hang about waiting to see him twice a month or whatever it is, the rest of your life is on hold, isn't it? I mean, don't you want children? I'm sorry to be brutal, but time isn't on your side. I imagine he'd be horrified if you got pregnant. Do you talk to him about it?'

'No. Of course it goes without saying that he doesn't want another child. I have thought about it, but I couldn't conceive without deceiving him. It would finish our affair and I don't want to be scrounging for maintenance all my life. When I have a baby, I want it to be wanted by its father too.'

'Well, I worry about you.'

'I know, Poppy. It's sweet of you to care, but I know what I'm doing, and so far I love it down here. But I do see what you mean. I wonder myself, when and where am I going to meet someone I want to marry? And who will want to marry me, more's to the point. What's the matter with me? Why haven't I found anyone? I used to have loads of blokes before.'

Poppy stretched out her lovely legs and leant back against the pub wall. 'Frankly, I think you are a less and less attractive proposition, Hatty, and I'm saying this because you know that I love you. Think of how a man is going to see you: you are a violin-teacher with no money, no career, still living like a student at nearly thirty-two. You don't have much to offer, do you? You can't cook, you don't have any wifely virtues that I can think of. Compare that to some bloody woman lawyer or corporate financier in designer clothes with a BMW and a flat in Chelsea and a great fat salary and pension. She can pretend she hasn't married because she has prioritised and that her career has had to come first. You don't have much to impress, do you? I know that you are still attractive. You've got lovely hair and a nice face, but it won't be long before the country life takes its toll and you'll be gallumphing around in puffa jackets and muddy trousers with broken veins in your ruddy cheeks, and I have to remind you again that you don't have youth on your side.'

'Poppy, you are foul. Why doesn't some man come along and love me for being me, just as I am? I'm not unlovable, am I? Lots of blokes have loved me in their time, but never the right one. I mean, I'd rather be single, like I am now, than put up with some nerd just for the sake of having a man.'

'Look, men in their thirties are different. They expect a woman of your age to have achieved. And you haven't. You'd seem like a bloody millstone. You've got to get going. Get a life. If you insist on teaching then it ought to be at the best school in the country, not at some ghastly all-female convent or whatever it is. I mean, who are you possibly going to meet there? A big co-ed public school would be a better hunting ground.'

'You make me feel utterly depressed. To go back to what men look for, why should a man want to take on one of these power-wielding women operating at permanently high stress levels and huge running costs? If I was a man I'd much prefer someone cheerful and easygoing and non-competitive like me. And I'm actually turning into a cook, I'll have you know. Before long I'll have a dinner party and you and Chris can come and admire my homely skills, and bring a rich banker who wants to marry a teapot-cosy sort of woman. Anyway, I remember you and Chris arguing about your career when he wanted you to give up and be a full-time wife and mother. So what do men want? You've contradicted yourself.'

'No, I haven't. Men are attracted to successful women who have made it in their own sphere. They marry them and then they want them to give it all up and subjugate themselves. If they earn enough they'd rather be the sole provider, I'm sure of it. It makes them feel empowered and in control. Anyway, what about Robert? Doesn't he want to keep things as they are? He doesn't want you to marry someone, does he? It's surely not in his interests.'

'Actually, I don't think he'd mind too much. I think he'd quite like to get me married off. But he would probably expect our present arrangement to go on unchanged.'

Poppy went off to the Ladies and left me sitting outside with Jess, feeling pretty depressed. She was gone for ages and when we went to look for her, she was playing a noisy game of pool with the Vested Ones. She had taken off her cardigan and tied it round her waist to hide the fact that her jeans were undone. She leaned over the table to take a shot and her bum was half the size of mine and looked pretty perfect. Jess and I stood and watched. Afterwards in the car Poppy said, 'Actually they were really rather sweet. The dark one, Jason, wants me to go back this evening.'

I stared at her in amazement. Poppy was from a different planet.

'Cheer up, Hazzy,' she said. 'You know, I really quite envy you. You are utterly free to be yourself. Look at me being a wife and a mother and an expectant mother and a daughter and a daughter-in-law . . . so many demands on me. Yes, I am much happier because I've grown up and realised that life is a compromise. Chris has done extremely well and I'm ashamed to say that this has made me conscious of what he is worth to me. I want to keep him and I want to keep him happy. I've met some of the single women he works with, like the ones I just described to you, and they are ruthless in pursuit of a decent man. They'd have me and Jess out on our ears if they sniffed any chance. You, at least, can be you.'

⬤═══⬤

I first told Poppy about my affair with Robert just after I'd discovered about Helen. I know how she would react and I felt so confused and hurt that I needed someone to confide in.

'Jesus!' said Poppy. 'The bastard! Doesn't it just make you sick? There he is, appearing oh so utterly respectable and well-respected, leading a double, no, triple, life. The hypocrisy of it! He keeps the little wife in Scotland warming his slippers . . . Oh no, he'd never divorce her. You bet he wouldn't. She'd take him to the cleaners and he'd lose his home and his housekeeper. Instead he opts for these extra-curricular activities where he lays down the ground rules and makes sure the bread is very well buttered on his side.'

'I know, I've thought that. But I can also see it from his point of view. What would be the point of breaking up his home? He's not desperately unhappy and he loves his children. Mary is mostly a very satisfactory wife it seems, who runs a highly efficient house. She just doesn't like sex. He says she's cold and unaffectionate but he doesn't want to smash up all that they have and start out again with somebody else. He's always said that isn't what he is looking for. There has never been any deception on his part. Both Helen and I accepted that from the start. It's true I didn't know about Helen and if I had, I probably wouldn't have started all this – although I would still have been flattered that he wanted me as well. She doesn't know about me and he says she'd give him up if she did. He doesn't want to lose her.'

'If he had to choose between you,' asked Poppy, 'who would it be?'

'I don't know,' I said. 'I'm too scared to ask. He said he was infatuated with her when she was young. He seems to deliberately tell me things like that. He says he won't ever love me, but oh God, Helen was different. She wouldn't have him then, of course. God, I hate her.'

'Well, I think you should tell him that you are not putting up with it any longer. Say that he has to choose, and then see what happens. After all, why should you share him? You are worth more than that. If he chooses Helen, then he's no good to you anyway, and you should get rid of him.'

So I did. The next time we met he brought some Scottish smoked salmon and a bottle of white wine from his cellar. Did Mary ever glance into his case and wonder? Apparently not. The bottle, naturally, came in a special insulated container that kept it at just the right temperature. Wasted really on me, who puts bottles for a quick chill in the freezer, or to warm in the bottom oven of the Rayburn. But Robert is a man who takes a great deal of trouble to do things properly. After we had made love and were lying comfortably in each other's arms and he was stroking my shoulder, I said, 'I've been thinking.'

'Oh dear.'

'Why oh dear?'

'Because in my experience, that opening generally presages trouble.'

'I want you to decide something.' I leant on my elbow so that I could watch his face. 'Are you ready? This is it then. It has got to be Helen or me. I'm not prepared to be second string. Much as I love all of this, it is spoilt for me because you leave me and go to someone else, and for all I know, do and say the same things to her.'

'I don't, as it happens – or at least only in a rudimentary way. I've told you I have a completely different relationship with her, but I understand what you say. May I think about it or do you want an answer now?' He was perfectly calm. He went on with his gentle stroking.

'No. Please think about it. When will you let me know?'

'I'll telephone you tonight.'

He was so unruffled and undisturbed and I wished then that I hadn't taken Poppy's advice. Poppy was too sure and confident with her dazzling looks and devoted husband. I had hoped the question would have raised more concern, would trouble him, but he was as cool as ever. We got dressed in a horrid detached way, hardly speaking, him throwing me my knickers which had gone under the bed, and straightening his tie in the glass. I hated saying goodbye. He kissed me briefly before sending me out into the corridor, with a farewell pat on my bottom, first looking both ways himself to check that all was clear.

He rang as usual at eleven-thirty. He said he was just about to go to bed at his club. He had thought about what I had said and his answer was no.

'No what?' I asked.

'No, I am not prepared to give up Helen.'

So I had my answer and had achieved nothing.

'Okay,' I said. 'Fine.' My voice indicated that this was not the truth.

'Darling, it's not fine, is it? It's bloody. I don't want to let you go, but I understand your feelings.'

'Yes,' I said.

'We'll keep in touch.'

And that was the first of our partings. I reported the next day to Poppy. If the arrangement he and I had arrived at was unsatisfactory it was as nothing to the misery I felt at having lost him.

'Why did you make me do it?' I wailed. 'Fat lot of good it's done me.'

'That's not true. You needed to know,' said Poppy. 'Now you can draw a line under R. Mackintosh. Begin again. Fresh page.'

I spent a miserable week or two moping about eating vast quantities and feeling my waistbands taking the strain. I lay in bed at night going through all our meetings, reliving every tender moment and feeling the desolation of my loss. Then I got an envelope through the post in his familiar handwriting. I felt weak with anticipation as I stood in the kitchen and held it in my hand. Inside was a single sheet of his expensive paper. On it was a four-line poem

> What's for me
> Without my Muse?
> Bottled beer
> And self-abuse?

You can guess that that started it all again.

And so it came to pass that I had to learn to accept Helen. I accepted her but I never stopped hating her. Robert and I had enough good times ourselves, and very few bad ones, for me to be able to push her to the back of my mind. I tried never to speak her name but her shadow was always there between us. I wondered when he saw her. How many times was he in London which I didn't know about? When he was on holiday in Spain, was he with her? I suspected he was. Mary would never go away in the growing season and they did not as a rule holiday together. He went to the opera festival in Wexford. Was she there? Once he came to London with blisters on his hands and a sunburned face. He'd been sailing, he said. Where? Oh, along the Suffolk coast.

She seemed to claim so much more of him than I did. She had so much more materially to offer. They met as equals. I imagined her pouring him malt whisky in a heavy cut-glass tumbler in a beamed sitting room. I could picture the tasteful room and the antiques and the level of graciousness. They were both used to lives made smooth by money. She met him once, I discovered, off a flight arriving at Heathrow. She was trying out her new car. What sort? 'Oh, a BMW, I think – very smart. Soft top. Great fun.' She took him to expensive restaurants, bought him presents. I noticed he was using a beautiful pen with a swirly enamelled case and gold nib. From Helen? He simply smiled. They had bought it together in the Burlington Arcade, where Helen had asked him to help her choose a cashmere sweater for herself.

Once he told me that she had booked a table for lunch at a smart new Conran restaurant she wanted to try. They made a mistake over their arrangements. She waited upstairs and he down and they didn't meet until they both got up to leave. Each had dined alone and with amusement he told me that they had both chosen the same dish – a risotto. They had laughed about it. It was the cheapest thing on the menu. Both Scots, you see. I felt hugely unamused. How could he relate this tale to me, redolent as it was with the special closeness that they shared? A lover's tale.

I started to suspect that the places he took me to were the same that Helen and he went to. For a month he was unusually available. Then I found out that Helen was away, walking in the Himalayas on some obscure expedition organised by a very exclusive specialist company, with the object of making the pampered and over-indulged traveller suffer expensively in remote corners of the world. 'Oh yes, she's a very adventurous girl,' he said fondly. *Girl!* I snorted. I collected all this information, mostly without comment, but I felt hot stabs of anger inside. I still didn't know her surname.

Once he told me that he had had a terrible row with her, really the worst row he had ever had with anyone. She had made him angrier than he had ever been before. I felt maddened by this power she had over him. With me he was always unmoved and mild. I wanted to know what the row had been about and he said that she had been up staying near his home in Scotland while Mary was away for a few days. They had spent the time together and one day she had started to comment on the sterility of his marriage, calling it a sham and a farce and insisting that Mary must know about her and simply chose to ignore the situation because she couldn't face a confrontation. She told him he lived a lie and that he was dishonourable and weak-willed. He should follow his heart and divorce Mary.

He was terribly angry and shouted at her and she had walked off – over, I suppose, the heather. Later they had had a sickening reconciliation and she told him he had misconstrued what she said. I pictured the whole scene in black and white, like an old film. Helen looked like Deborah Kerr and was wearing a twinset. Robert, in baggy tweed trousers, seized her by the arms in a masterful way while the background of heathery moor became misty with intensity and grey storm clouds raced across the sky above.

'Were you angry because some of what she said is true?' I asked.

He looked at me for a long moment. 'Probably,' he said.

The only satisfaction I got out of any of this was that know-it-all Helen, so sure of her ground, so condescending to Mary, so pleased with her own superiority, was ignorant of me. I knew that somehow this gave me some power over her, but I couldn't see how I could use it. Then one day Robert wrote me a note on the back of a print-out. He often used scrap paper in this way – another Scottish trait, I suppose. I turned the sheet over and studied the printing. It was an itemised telephone bill of about twenty numbers. It didn't take me long to work my way through them. Eight were London numbers, and I recognised mine and also his office. I saw with satisfaction that he spoke to me for twenty minutes. I rang the others and found that one was his son, who worked in London. I listened to his answerphone message: he had the same voice as his father. Another was a business number. That left two others and the out-of-town exchanges. One of these had been called twice on one day. I rang the operator and she told me that the exchange was Southwold, Suffolk. Ah! Success at last!

I looked closely at the times the calls were made. A minute before the Suffolk number had first been rung, he had tried a London number with no success. Again I rang the operator. The exchange was Hampstead. I dialled the number and got an answerphone message. It was a breathy, middle-class female voice saying that no one was available to take the call. I rang the Suffolk number, some instinct making me use the secrecy prefix of 141. It was answered on the third ring. 'Haylo?' The same voice.

'Helen?' I asked.

'Yes, who is it?' I rang off. Thank God she couldn't call me back. I felt a criminal already.

Now I had traced Helen I had to be careful. I couldn't allow myself to indulge in too many mysterious telephone calls or I would arouse her suspicions and she'd tell the police or change her number. I had to ration myself. Only very rarely did I ring and put the receiver down after she'd answered. Once or twice I affected an accent and pretended I had dialled a wrong number. It gave me a weird feeling to actually speak to her. Once I telephoned and asked to speak to a fictitious Michael.

'I think you must have a wrong number,' she said. She sounded annoyed.

'Oh, I am sorry.'

'Michael who?' she asked, as if there was a chance that she might know who I wanted. It was somehow typical of Helen to believe that she had special encyclopaedic knowledge of the entire London telephone directory.

'Michael O'Ryan,' I made up on the spur of the moment. She had taken me completely by surprise by asking me questions.

'No. You have a wrong number,' she confirmed. 'What number did you have for him?'

I repeated her own, but changed two of the digits.

'You have dialled the number wrongly,' she reprimanded me. Afterwards I marvelled at how bossy and managing she was. Most people would simply say, 'Wrong number,' and hang up. She somehow turned a misdialled code into an inquisition. Later I got Loops to telephone and ask to speak to Belinda, her daughter.

'She's not in,' said Helen. 'Who is that?'

'Just a friend,' said Loops dreamily.

'Yes, but what name?' demanded Helen.

Loops said, 'Byeee. Give her my love,' and rang off. 'God!' she said. 'What a Gestapo cow!'

What was most useful was that I could now check on my suspicions that Robert and Helen were away together. When he was in New York for ten days, she too was away. He telephoned me the day he got back, and we met the following afternoon. Helen was also home the same day. I knew because I telephoned her number and her line was engaged. Sometimes when he had to leave me to go to evening functions in London, I would telephone her London number and find that she was there. Once I was sure that I heard his voice in the background. None of this activity made things any better but somehow made me feel I was tracking a situation in which I was otherwise helpless. It was Loops who dealt the master stroke and found out Helen's surname. I had made her ring one night when I was particularly suspicious that Robert had left me early to go and join her.

'Hi,' said Loops when the telephone was answered. 'Can I speak to Fi?' All Loops's friends, either real or fictitious, have strange abbreviated names.

'Oh!' she said after a pause. 'Well, what number have I got then? Who am I speaking to?'

She came off the phone, smiling triumphantly. 'Caplan,' she said. 'She said her name was Belinda Caplan. It must have been the daughter in person. She's much nicer than her mother. Must take after her dad.'

Helen Caplan. Now I can hate you by name.

★   ★   ★

Robert knew nothing of all this. I made a point of being as casual as possible about Helen, lulling him into believing that I accepted the situation meekly. He couldn't have known of my hideous plots to wipe her off the face of the earth, nor how much she occupied my private thoughts. I longed to see her, not to meet her but just to observe her without her knowing she was watched. Smug and assured, confident that she occupied a world that she controlled by money and position, she would be dogged by an unseen menace.

Loops thought I was going mad. 'I'll be your contract killer,' she said. 'It would be quite a laugh. I could strangle her in a lift in Harrods or push her under a Tube train. Don't you ever think how easy that would be when you are on a platform in the rush hour?'

'I bet she goes everywhere by taxi,' I said. Loops was joking, mucking about. She didn't realise how deadly serious I was.

Chapter Seven

Term started at my school in Salisbury. I had to go in for a staff meeting and spent the evening before sorting through my clothes for something respectable to wear. I ended up in a long black skirt that I used for performances and a white shirt which I ironed. Feeling appropriately demure and plain I packed Pilgrim into my car and drove to start my new profession.

It was all very much as I had expected, and indeed, very much like the day school I myself had attended in London. The staff were unmistakably teachers. Of course, they were all shapes and sizes and there were one or two men among them, but on the whole they were middle-aged or older women of uniform drabness. There were some arty ones with draped scarves and more flowing garments who clearly did not wish to be mistaken for dull scientists, but most of them seemed to have thick, serviceable ankles and wore large, flat shoes. Some had hoisted little flags of courage – touches of colour in bright cardigans, or pink lipstick or green eyeshadow. All wore tights, even though it was still August. I felt underdressed with my bare legs and sandals, and I did up another button on my shirt.

There was a lot of fussing about with lists and timetables. No one took much notice of me because part-time music staff occupy a dim hinterland generally unpenetrated by the rest of the teachers. My head of department, an energetic woman in her fifties called Miss Arthur, was friendly and encouraging and I met the other members of the department who were also welcoming. One or two I had already encountered professionally or knew of, and we indulged in the closed chit-chat of the performing world. I was allocated some class teaching and several individual pupils, and was pleased with the prospect of being busy again. We had a cafetière of coffee in the music office and Miss Arthur produced a bag of doughnuts. There was a lot of talking and laughing and the man who taught brass created a cheerful atmosphere with his frequent booming laugh. I drove home feeling pleased with my career decision and looking forward to starting the next day.

That first school term wore on, and as September changed into winter, I gradually became used to my new life, although for a long time I hated coming back in the dark and felt terrified as I paused by the door, fumbling with my key. The country night was too huge and wide and empty, and it seemed more threatening to me than a busy London street lit with street-lamps and full of traffic and people. I felt terribly alone. The country was no place for single people. Neighbouring cottages were brightly lit and warm with families. Even those which stood empty during the week came alive with couples and children at the weekend. The groups gathered at the bus stop in the village in the mornings as I drove through, were young mothers seeing older children onto the school bus or pushing toddlers and smaller children up to the primary school in Cow Path Lane. Laughing and talking to one another, their children running and whooping ahead of them, they belonged to a group from which I was excluded. Quite a lot of them looked younger than me, barely out of their teens with long hair and high-heeled boots and studs in their noses. Most of these families lived in the small council estate behind the shop. The fathers worked on the land or were drivers for MilkMarque, or drove every day to the industrial estate in the nearest market town. I'd seen them on Saturday afternoons tinkering with their clapped-out cars, their children circling the cul de sacs on bicycles.

The other group of mothers I noticed in the mornings were those involved in the school run to the local prep school. They drove too fast down the lanes in their estate cars packed with children, sweeping into gravelled drives to collect Sophie or Charlie and have a shouted conversation with another mother who had come to the door in jeans and untidy hair, holding a coffee mug. I caught glimpses of these lives as I drove past their large houses or restored cottages, but they did not touch my own.

I realised that bedsit land on the fringes of cities is the natural habitat of the single unattached female, where being on your own is less extraordinary and remarked on, where you can join groups of people in pubs, cinemas and clubs and walk singly along a street at night without drawing attention to yourself. Here, in the country, I was unusual . . . living alone in my cottage, keeping the world from my door like a witch from the past. An outsider, I could not be absorbed by the young families because I had nothing in common with them; I was totally out of step with the rhythm of their lives. How, I wondered, had single women lived in the days when Jerusalem Farm supported a family, when the tiny second bedroom was warmed by the bodies of sleeping children sharing a bed? How had the spinsters of this parish fitted into the community? If they had not been born with the advantages of wealth and position, they would have earned their keep much as today. The village schoolteacher was often a Miss. I imagined that she would have had an established place in the rural community, along with unmarried seamstresses, cooks, farmhands and shopkeepers. Established at the bottom of the table, that is. The least regarded, the least respected. The unchosen ones. But here I was, solitary by choice, leading an independent life, at a price. Unlike my sisters of the past I could be flexible, unattached, opportunistic. Within the restraints imposed by my work, I could do and be as I wished and I would therefore never belong. I was like a migrating bird blown off course.

To begin with I felt nervous every time I went out. I bought an OS map and set about discovering footpaths which networked the fields and woods. When I got in from work the evenings were still light and the beautiful tranquil countryside beckoned. However, I felt constantly jumpy and on edge. Every deserted track seemed to hold a hidden menace, every bush a dark hiding place for a rapist or a mugger. The woods were full of shifting sounds of stirred branches, the empty fields desolate and forbidding. It took me weeks to feel less menaced and for the surrounding country to seem familiar and comforting. Gradually I began to know the trees. At the corner of this path stood an old oak whose twisted knotted branches looked like hands. Here was the hedge full of delicious brambles in September. I picked enough to make six pots of jam. Here the grassy bank where the evening sun filtered through the hazel thicket. To my unobservant city eyes a tree was a tree, but I was learning to distinguish one from another.

There was also an extraordinary amount of carnage to get used to. Pilgrim caught rabbits and brought their limp flopping bodies back to me. Thank God he always killed them outright. Sometimes they had gummed up, blistered eyes and I realised that they were blinded by myxomatosis. I got used to seeing squashed badgers on the lane, their sensitive-looking feet and strong claws helplessly turned to the sky. I saw a ewe in a field, quietly grazing while from her back end trailed a mass of blood and matter. I saw crows pulling at the entrails of dead sheep; a half-dead lamb with its eyes pecked out.

And yet I enjoyed the change from London, the different pace, the chance to be alone. I began to treat myself to small indulgences. A special piece of steak, a rug for my bedroom floor, flowers for the kitchen table, a long Saturday morning in bed with tea, the radio and Pilgrim. Much of the pressure and frustration of my old life had been removed. Mostly I felt peaceful, but the Furies were not banished completely and Helen was never far from my thoughts. I could make my life enjoyable, pleasurable with minor satisfactions but there always lurked the threat of the mood that sometimes beset me and which could render everything I had and did empty, pointless, worthless.

Pilgrim saved me from myself. Having him there made all the difference. I thought of my mother who had never once complained of nerves or loneliness over all the years she has lived alone, and felt proud of her. I thought of her in power cuts and storms and being woken by an unfamiliar noise in the night, and I felt ashamed at my lack of concern for her. I was acutely conscious of my isolation and often lay rigid with fear as the cottage creaked and groaned in the night. I dragged Pilgrim's bed up the stairs but if I let him into my room he somehow managed to end up on the bed, or else kept me awake with systematic licking or snoring which drove me mad. I banished him to guard the landing outside my door, but he wasn't having that and simply went downstairs and scratched and whined to be let back into the kitchen where it was warmer.

As the weeks wore on I got used to the solitary life and became less fearful. I felt as if the cottage had accepted me, enfolded me. The dark was no longer menacing. I could go downstairs at night for a glass of water without turning on the light. I knew the feel of the bannisters, the angle of the stairs. I began to find the noise of the old timbers settling more comforting than frightening. Whatever spirits I shared the cottage with were on my side.

My mother found me some lovely faded old curtains at a jumble sale. They were thick with interlining and she knelt on the floor and pinned and hemmed them so that they fitted my sitting-room windows, when they were drawn. They closed me in as effectively as double glazing. She also gave me some furniture she had in store and best of all, my father's old desk.

'He wanted you to have it. Strange, really, when you were the least academic.'

I got used to leaving the key to the kitchen door under a stone and she came and went when I was at work. I often found a vase of flowers or a loaf of home-made bread on the table with a note to say that she had called.

The other source of pleasure was the old cream-coloured stove. I scraped away at the dirt and grease and got off most of the rusty stains. I learned how to manage its appetite for fuel and knew that if I treated it right it would glow steadily day and night, and be warm and comforting on the chilly mornings, so much so that Pilgrim wouldn't go out when I came down to make my tea, but snuggled deeper into his bed and pretended he didn't hear me call. I bought cheap cuts of meat and simmered them all day, so that when I got home in the evening there was a delicious smell; I opened the oven door, and supper would be waiting. I experimented with bread-making, and although the pile of wholemeal bricks in the garden grew where I had thrown them in disgust – I'll make a wall with them, I thought, an organic, wholemeal wall – I eventually met with success and produced something not only edible but delicious.

When I invited Poppy and Chris for the weekend, Poppy said, 'God! No thanks. What would we do surrounded by wet fields, and those great flocks of cows and bulls breathing BSE? Well, we might come for the day. I'm so bloody enormous you'll have to move the furniture to get me in.' So they did and I cooked roast beef from the village butcher and Chris raved about it and Poppy lay on the sofa by the fire and went to sleep and Chris, Jess and I took Pilgrim for a walk along the bridle path through the woods. Chris tucked my arm through his and I held Jess's hand and he remarked on how well I looked and what a lovely place I had found to live.

'I think it's such a good thing that you've made a break from London. All this is so settled, so healthy – it really suits you.' Our breath puffed in clouds and the woods smelt damp and mouldy. The sun set in a sky streaked with red. I felt very happy. Chris said he'd love to move out of London, particularly now with another baby coming, but Poppy couldn't stand the idea of being stuck in the country while he worked City hours away from home. He looked a bit wistful and sad, so I changed the subject and made him collect kindling for the fire, and he set to and got a great wet armful and said he loved the idea of being a hunter-gatherer. It started to get dark very quickly and we stood listening, entranced, to the owls hooting across the valley.

When we got back I promised Jess chocolate biscuits for tea and she ran on to wake up Poppy. Chris held me back by the kitchen door. He kissed me on the lips and said, 'Oh Hazzy!' which, when I thought about it after they'd gone, I put down to pre-natal strain. I smiled in a non-conspiratorial way. 'You're a soppy old thing. Poppy, you've got a soppy husband! He thinks he wants to snog me,' I shouted through the door.

'Oh, please let him. He hasn't been able to get near me for weeks.'

I kissed his cheek and hurried in to put the kettle on. It was easy to make a joke out of it.

★ ★ ★

Robert continued to keep in touch much as he had before. He had suggested mildly that my moving to Somerset might make meeting more difficult, but so far it hadn't really proved to be so. Of course, now that I had regular work I couldn't meet him for long afternoons of love, but there were the holidays and weekends. I went five weeks without seeing him and then saw him three times in five days. I could catch the train at Salisbury and be in London one and a half hours later.

My dear mother was most obliging and took Pilgrim for me. I had to be cagey about what I was doing and who with, and felt bad when she said, 'I'm delighted to help. I worry that you don't see enough of your friends. Anyway, Pilgrim is no bother. I enjoy having him. He's such a peaceful sort of dog.'

We had a family Christmas that year. My sister Isabel, an efficient housekeeper, successful barrister and mother of three boys aged twelve, nine and seven, had us all to stay in her big house in Richmond. There were sixteen of us altogether and it was noisy and fun. Loops and I slept on futons and talked half the night. I had a time arranged on Christmas Day when I could ring Robert, who was at home in Scotland. I'd given him some shooting stockings in a poisonous pond green which, if he ever wore them, would make him look like Jeremy Fisher. They had come from a terrible 'County' shop in Salisbury where the staff were so busy proving that they were not shopkeeper class that they could hardly bring themselves to serve the customers.

He and I had met the week before in London and he'd given me a book for Christmas, an anthology of women travel writers. We'd had a lovely afternoon in bed and then I had watched him getting dressed to go to a dinner in a velvet dinner jacket. He had to make a speech and had bought himself a silk bow tie and matching handkerchief from a very grand London shop. As he drew them out of a deliciously glamorous carrier bag and unwrapped them from layers of tissue paper, I couldn't help but think of how that particular shop stocked beautiful and luxurious lingerie as well. He hummed to himself as he adjusted his appearance in the mirror and sleeked back his patrician mane of hair, turning his head this way and that. He's not a vain man but his appearance is a comfort to him. He turned to me, still lying naked in his bed and smiled affectionately.

'You'll have to get up, sweetie.' I climbed out and went across the room, naked, to have a shower. As I came out he was waiting for me with a glass of wine in his hand. The towel dropped off my pink, steamy body as I took the glass. He patted my bottom. 'My lovely Rubens bather,' he said.

I thought about this as I dialled his number in my brother-in-law's study. Jake is a scientific journalist and lives in a state of chaos with books and papers exploding off every surface. I stirred some of the rubbish round with my foot as the telephone rang.

Robert answered at once. 'Happy Christmas, sweetie. How are you?' I told him about our Christmas and thanked him for the book. 'What about you?' I asked.

'Mary loves to do a family thing, so there's . . . about twenty-five of us, and then we're having our usual party tomorrow lunchtime. We have about sixty people to drinks and then the best of them stay to lunch.' My heart sank. I could just picture it all. It was all so complete without me, so utterly unassailable. Here I was, on the fringes of my sister's life, sharing her family, still in the wings. There he was, centre stage, playing the lead in the drama of his life. I imagined him in a new cashmere sweater Mary had given him, checking wine and bringing in logs, perhaps dozing in an armchair after lunch. I ached to be part of the little, insignificant, domestic moments. Because I was banished from that part of his life, it seemed infinitely desirable.

I'd sometimes tell him this and he'd say, 'Don't be silly, sweetie. I can promise you that you see the best of me. I'm a grumpy old fart most of the time at home.'

'Where's Helen?' I asked.

'Oh, in Suffolk with her children. She's going away skiing in the New Year.'

'What did she give you?' Why, oh why, did I do it to myself?

'Something rather super, actually. She's bought us tickets for the Salzburg season.'

'Happy Christmas, Jeremy Fisher,' I said, and gently put down the receiver.

He didn't ring back. I sat for a moment with my head in my hands at Jake's desk, wallowing in misery, until Loops put her head round the door.

'Fucking Christmas spirit!' she said. 'Come on, we want you for charades.'

I drove my mother home after Christmas with the car full of presents and leftover food and Pilgrim, who I had discovered is an appalling thief. He'll eat virtually anything if it's stolen. It was therefore no mean feat to separate him from mince pies and cold turkey and ham for the duration of the journey.

I had a real sense of returning home as we went west and the country changed from suburbia to the rolling downs and wide vistas before Stonehenge. I delivered my mother back to her cottage and together we turned up the heating and put the water back on; checked everything was all right. There were a few late Christmas cards on the mat and a cup and saucer from her last cup of coffee, neatly rinsed and left to dry on the draining board. Apart from that everything was utterly ready for her to resume life there. She is really so much more competent than me.

'Will you be all right, darling? Would you like to stay

the night here?' She still treated me as a protective parent might a fragile child.

'No, of course not. I'm fine. Thanks, anyway, mother of mine. If you're okay, I'll go now and get back before it's dark.'

'Of course – you do that. It's been a lovely Christmas, hasn't it? A proper family affair.'

She insisted that I take some milk and bread from her freezer. When I got back to Jerusalem Farm, Pilgrim stood up in the car for the last few yards, and shivered with pleasure. That didn't last long because, of course, the stove was out and the cottage felt icily damp and cold. I unloaded the stuff from the car into the middle of the sitting room but didn't feel like unpacking. I'd left in a hurry and clothes and shoes were all over the place and the kitchen floor was dirty. There were dirty plates in the sink and a dish left to soak.

Pilgrim hunched his bony back and stared gloomily at a spot on the carpet, shaking in an exaggerated way. I wrapped him in a blanket but he wouldn't co-operate and cheer up and stood like a shivering clothes horse in silent reproach. The cottage felt eerily empty. I put on all the lights and the television, opened a bottle of chilly wine a parent from school had given me for Christmas and tried to light the stove. The wood was damp and the nuggets of coal would not catch. Pilgrim began to whimper.

'Sod and fuck and fuck it and sod it!' I screamed. I threw down a handful of twigs onto the floor. I was too cold to cry.

'Want some help?' said a voice from outside the window.

<hr>

The Rubens bather remark was one of a series of similar comments which I was getting used to. Robert is not given to compliments. He reminds me of the Stanley character played by Marlon Brando in *A Streetcar Named*

Desire who says, 'A broad says to me, "I'm the glamorous type" and I say, "So what? So what if you're the
glamorous type?" ', or something like that. He seemed
to take it for granted that the greatest compliment he
could pay me was his interest in me and that therefore
nothing extra was required. He rarely said that I looked
beautiful, or that he liked what I was wearing, or that I
had lovely hair, teeth, eyes, whatever. Mostly I had to
ask him.

'Do you like me in this colour? Don't you think it's a
lovely blue?' I desperately wanted his approbation but
he rarely gave it.

'You don't need to be told you're attractive,' he said.
Much more often he teased me about my big feet or my
Bohemian style of clothes as he called it. 'It's Boho chic,'
I told him.

'Oh, is it? Very curious. You mean you can buy this
sort of thing,' indicating a velvet skirt I was wearing, 'in
shops?'

'God! You're so bloody rude!' I said.

'I don't desire you for your sartorial elegance,' he
said. 'Come here – you are much better without your
clothes. You can't blame me for thinking that.'

I complained to Poppy. 'It's obvious,' she said, pulling a
great dark nipple from her new baby's mouth with a
slurping noise and passing his little downy head to her
right side, where he latched onto her like a Hoover
attachment and began an industrious sucking and
gulping.

'What do you mean?'

'Well, you're looking for a father figure, aren't you?
Your father died when you were eighteen. You're in
love with a man nearly the age he would have been
now. You're desperate to please him, for him to want
you and admire you.'

'I know. It's so obvious that I've thought of all that,

80

but it's not true. He's nothing like my father – couldn't be less like him, in fact. My dad was sort of other-worldly and tremendously upright and moral. He'd never have got tangled up in the web of deceit that Robert lives with. My father completely suppressed his physical appetites, I think. His passion was for Virgil, Ovid and stuff. He wept as he read the death of Socrates to us. He was entirely cerebral. And another thing . . . when he died we all felt a tremendous loss, of course, but his love for us was so complete that we didn't feel we'd missed anything. His love was never conditional on us being clever or musical or attractive. We all felt utterly loved just for how we were. His life was too short and it was terrible when he died, but he didn't leave us damaged by dying then. That's not his legacy. I won't have it that it is.'

'Come here, dearie,' said Pops, 'let me kiss you,' and she pulled my face down to her and kissed my cheek while little Tom, eyes shut and a look of bliss on his face, caressed her breast with a tiny starfish hand and ceased his sucking to fall into rapturous sleep.

'Get rid of him,' she said later as we sat with mugs of tea and a packet of shortbread biscuits. 'Either get rid of him, or stop caring so much. You're too fucking good for him, anyway.'

'Yes,' I said. 'Maybe I will. Let Helen have him. Winner takes all.'

I couldn't bear it that Helen didn't suffer as I did. I imagined that her affair was entirely satisfactory to her. Robert adored her. She basked in the warmth of his affection. He couldn't marry her which was annoying, but apart from that she benefited from all the advantages of having a lover, with none of the agony of knowing she was not the only one. I imagined her patting on her face cream in the mornings, looking into the glass and seeing a beautiful woman with a face, skin, eyes, teeth, a mouth, that Robert loved and covered in kisses. As she brushed her hair she would watch the light falling on its marmalade tones and know that he loved redheads above all others. She would dress knowing that her figure was endlessly exciting to him. Her breasts, her shoulders, her hips, thighs . . . all admired, held, stroked. He had lit up her life with the glow of his admiration, the heady pleasure that comes from being desired above all others, of being the chosen one. The hurt of her straying husband was dissolved in Robert's attentions to her.

She was being cheated but it didn't matter because she didn't know. I was the one who knew, and the truth brought me no pleasure but ate away at the affection Robert afforded me. The truth for me was that I felt permanently a second choice. What I saw in the mirror was a face he found less touching than Helen's; my breasts and thighs; the sex I opened my legs for him to enjoy; all less attractive to him than Helen's. I had been judged and put into second place. But when I was with him, lying in his arms after a glorious time of released physical passion and he was holding me tenderly, I couldn't believe this was true. He'd made love to me with such careful attention, groaned with such intensity, came with such a shout of relief and release that the experience was complete and wonderful in itself and could not be held up for comparison. I didn't care then how he felt about Helen. He fucked me as if I was the only woman in the world.

'You're the most delicious girl,' he said, 'and I am a lucky and undeserving man.'

That was how he saw it. Simple. He liked having us both.

The face at my kitchen window that night after Christmas nearly made me faint with shock. Pressed against the glass it looked the stuff of horror films, distorted and fishily pale. Almost as soon as I had screamed, I realised it was Toby. I opened the door.

'Fuck you, Toby! I nearly died of fright. What are you doing out there in the dark?'

'I saw your light on as I was coming down the lane. Thought I'd see if everything was okay. I knew you were coming back this evening and I was going to ask you if you'd like to come out for a drink. Sorry if I scared you. I seem to have interrupted a moment of significant stress.'

'Jesus! You frightened me. Look at me – I'm ashen. God! I need a drink.' I poured him a glass of cold red wine and gulped my own. 'Sorry. It's at room temperature, which as you'll notice is bloody freezing. I can't get the stove to light.'

'Here, let me have a go,' said dear Toby. He took off his tweed jacket and squatted in front of the stove in his woolly jumper. His rugby thighs bulged in his cord trousers.

'You're very Boden catalogue,' I said, looking at him and slurping the wine which had already gone to my head. ' "Toby, estate manager, in corn-coloured cords and dove-grey sweater." Christmas presents?' Did he have a girlfriend who dressed him as a toff? I wondered.

'No,' he said, quite coldly. 'Stop sneering at me, if you want me to go on with this.'

That set me back on my heels. 'What do you mean, sneering? I'm not sneering.'

'Well, it sounds as if you are. All you bloody London people. You are so up yourselves. This is just what I wear because it's what I'm comfortable in. Okay?'

'*Okay!* Don't be cross. I promise I didn't mean to sneer. For God's sake look at me.' I indicated my jeans and sweater, topped by a mangy fake fur coat of Loops'. 'How could anyone, looking quite so disastrous as me, sneer at how someone else is dressed? Toby, it really upsets me that you think I would.'

'Oh, shut up,' he said as the fire in the stove leapt and lit up his face. He dropped a few more bits of coal on and shut the door, opening the damper. In a few seconds we could hear the roar as it took hold. I refilled his glass.

'Thank you *so* much,' I said sincerely. 'Sit down.' I looked at him, assessing his age. Thirty-three? I knew he wasn't married. I also knew with a horrible certainty that I didn't find him attractive. He was nice, however, and he'd lit my stove. I began to put away the stuff lying on the floor. Pilgrim crept onto his bean bag by the stove.

'Could you bear some cold ham and turkey and all that post-Christmas wreckage?' I asked. 'I can put some pots in to bake and they'd be done by the time we got back from the pub, or would you rather just stay here? I've got a bottle of port somewhere. It will soon warm up and I can light the sitting-room fire.'

He leant back in the kitchen armchair. 'What a good idea! I'd much rather stay here. It's time we got to know one another, don't you think?'

Chapter Eight

Toby and I got fabulously drunk the night he came to visit me. We drank the wine I'd opened and then Toby fetched another bottle he had in his car. We ate cold turkey, ham and chutney with the bread my mother had given me, and then we started on the port. I had drawn the curtains and the cottage was warm and friendly again. It had come back to me and felt quite different from the icy stranger which had cold-shouldered me a few hours before.

To begin with, Toby and I were both awkward, not knowing one another well enough to be able to relax. Conversation was stilted until the wine began to work and the atmosphere became easier. I felt all the time there was a sub-text. We were both single and about the same age, and these facts loomed suggestively over us and could not be ignored. Sooner or later this ground was going to have to be covered.

I lit candles and we sat on the floor by the sitting-room fire and talked. Toby knew a huge amount about the area because he had grown up nearby and had been to school in Devon. His family still farmed in the next valley. He told me how much he loved it, and when I pointed out the shortcomings to him, especially how isolated it was if one was single, he told me that that was my fault, and that there was masses going on if one took the trouble to look.

I envied him his sense of belonging – he knew everyone – and his passion for the place. He said he envied me my music. After a while he persuaded me to play him a few pieces on the violin . . . some lovely Polish Christmas carols with haunting melodies . . . and then he admitted that he could play the piano. He asked me if I'd do some music with him in the church, and at the parish supper in the village hall on Twelfth Night. I was not very keen.

'I'm a professional,' I complained. 'I have to try and make a living out of playing.'

'Professionals do offer their services to the community, you know,' he reproved me. 'Accountants do the parish books, a lawyer looks after the legal stuff . . .'

'Okay, okay,' I said. 'Point taken. I'm just not used to this community thing. Where I come from, it's every man for himself.'

I asked him more about the village and particularly about Jerusalem Farm. I wanted to know whose spirits haunted it.

'There's something here, you know, Toby. Really. I know it sounds silly, but I never feel alone. I'm sharing this place with someone. It's not bad or menacing or evil . . . nothing like that. I'd just like to know who it is.' I thought he might laugh but he didn't.

'I don't know anything further back than the last ten years or so, when it has been let to London people like you. But there's a history of the village which you can get at the local shop. It's rather a good book, well-researched, all profits to the village funds. There'll be something in there about it. But now I want to know more about you.'

'I've been avoiding this. I'm not very good at talking about myself. What do you want to know?'

'Well, for a start, why are you here?'

And so I went through it all, leaving out any reference to relationships.

'Are you married?' asked Toby.

'God, no! Look, no ring!'

'That doesn't mean anything. You easily might have been. Not divorced either?'

'No. Unattached and unscathed,' I replied lightly. Robert had nothing to do with this. 'What about you?' I asked, and was totally taken aback when Toby said that he'd been married for five years, and was divorced.

'Jesus! Sorry, I don't mean to be rude, but you look too young to have been through all that,' I said.

'Sadly not,' said Toby. He looked into the fire. It was easier to talk that way, in the comforting darkness of the room. 'No, I was married to a local girl, Susie, a farmer's daughter. We'd known one another for years. She's a very keen rider – eventing, hunting, that sort of thing – and after a while I could see I was losing her. She had moved into another world. We had an agonising year or so, or at least I did, and then she told me she wanted to leave me. She lives with David Middleton, the Master of Hounds. It's okay now. I mean, I see her often, inevitably. It's a chapter closed. I've moved on.'

'Toby, I'm so sorry. How horrible for you.'

He shrugged. 'A lot of it was my fault, I can see that. I couldn't keep up with the life she wanted and, really, I didn't want to. It's taken me a while to deal with the jealousy I felt, but I seem to have managed, and I don't think about it all the time like I used to.'

'Do you still love her?'

Toby looked up. His heavy, round face wore a troubled expression. 'I don't think so, not now. I can look back and know I did then, when we were married, but I can't let myself go on loving her or it will destroy me. I loved her most when I was losing her. That was the worst part.'

'Yes, I can imagine. I think it always is. Aren't you lonely? Have you gone back to living on your own?'

'Yes, of course I am at times, but I'm a pretty

self-sufficient person. I did most of the cooking anyway. I still live in the cottage we shared. Susie was the one who moved out. I've just got used to it. You can't change what you can't alter.'

'Yes, I know,' I said.

'I do have a little more self-respect than I did then. I look back and realise that when I suspected something was going on, I was too scared to confront it. I chose to ignore the fact that she had probably been in bed all afternoon with David because I didn't want to lose her. It was easier to try and pretend the situation was bearable. Which it wasn't. It was an awful state of limbo, of no-man's-land. I was eaten away by suspicion and jealousy. And then things would be better and I'd convince myself that it was just me, imagining things. I'm glad in a way that she brought it to an end and gave me a chance of freeing myself, too. But first I had to fight the feeling of failure. My parents couldn't believe it had happened. They somehow implied it was due to an inadequacy on my part. They've never had a very high opinion of me and they really liked Susie. As time went by, I began to see that the break-up was inevitable and that it wasn't because I'd failed in some way. She had just stopped loving me and wanted someone else who suited her better. She had changed and I couldn't, however hard I tried, be the person she wanted.'

'Oh shit! Toby, you poor sod.' I reached out for his hand and squeezed it.

'It was pretty bloody at the time, but as I say, it's all water under the bridge.'

Tentatively, my tongue loosened by the wine and a feeling of comradeship after Toby's revelations, I told him that I was trying to get a disastrous affair into perspective. 'It's going nowhere, but it's impossible to stop,' I confided.

'Nonsense,' said Toby. 'It's not impossible. It would be easy if you wanted.' I did not feel like exploring this avenue. I wanted sympathy, not a talking-to.

'Are you going out with anyone?' I asked him.

'No, not seriously. I don't particularly want to yet. I don't feel whole enough, somehow.'

'That's exactly how I feel! If I attempt another friendship, I feel as if I'm only half there,' I said.

'Well, why don't the two halves of us go out occasionally?' asked Toby.

'I'd love to!' I really meant it. 'And you can introduce me to everyone you know. There might be some man lurking out there who'd take me on.'

'He'd be a lucky chap,' said Toby stoutly.

At that moment the telephone rang. I knew who it would be and rushed into the kitchen to answer it. I didn't want to expose my feebleness with Robert in front of Toby. As I picked up the receiver and said, 'Hello,' the receiver at the other end was slowly put down. Puzzled, I dialled 1471. The number had been withheld. A moment later it rang again, and the performance was repeated.

'Odd,' I said to Toby, as I described the calls.

'Some nutter,' he shrugged and topped up my glass. After that we got very drunk and I remember very little else. Toby slept on the floor under a quilt and I went up to bed. The next day we both felt deservedly ghastly. We couldn't bear to speak to one another but a bond had been forged and Toby and I were friends. A few days later he telephoned and organised a rehearsal for the musical entertainment in the village hall. I was being drawn in, and I felt guardedly pleased.

The next time I was in the village shop I saw, on the counter, a pile of the local history books Toby had mentioned. I picked up a copy and flicked through the pages. There were a lot of grainy black and white photographs and detailed accounts of the parish with each property described. It seemed to cover ancient history, through Domesday to the World Wars and the present day. I bought a copy. £10 seemed a bit steep but the proceeds were for the benefit of the village and the book clearly represented a huge amount of careful research. I didn't have a chance to look at it until that evening when I was sitting in my kitchen armchair with a glass of wine and Pilgrim at my feet. It took me a while to find the right page, and then I read;

Jerusalem Farm. Parts of this small farmhouse are over 300 years old. Mrs Lucy Sharpstone writing in 1964 to the then owners, Mr and Mrs Foote, described what the cottage was like in her early childhood in the 1890s. There was a kitchen, a sitting room, a workshop, a cellar, a vegetable garden, a pigsty, a stable and, in the field behind the cottage, a cow shed. The existence of a cellar with an outside trapdoor and a stone rampway, down which barrels could be rolled, adds the suggestion that it could have been an alehouse at some time. Mrs Sharpstone's brother, Thos. Frost, who was in the church choir at the time of Queen Victoria's Golden Jubilee in 1887, remembered the cellar being always full of potatoes and other things. The cottage belonged to the Frost family for nearly 200 years. In 1848 it was owned by them and a Henry Frost was the occupier. According to the 1851 census, he had a wife Betsy and three sons and three daughters. By 1891 we have one main household, that of Alice Frost aged 29, a widow with six children, the youngest called Lucy (Mrs Sharpstone?). Mrs Sharpstone wrote that they left the cottage when her mother died in about 1895. Sometime between the 1850s and 1890s the farm was acquired by the Harston Estate. The first tenants were mainly estate workers.

I took a sip of wine and thought about widowed Alice and her family. How the rooms must have rung with voices, how booted feet must have clattered up and down my stairs. How exhausted she must have been as she sat in this kitchen in the evenings by the light of an oil lamp. How she must have worked to put food on the table for six children. I thought of the aching winter cold and the damp, and wet clothes and muddy boots. What relentless drudgery. At twenty-nine, did she have any memories of her youth and beauty left? How flimsy and superficial it made my life and my preoccupations seem by contrast. My thoughts were broken by the telephone. When I answered it the line went dead. I telephoned Robert. For once he was there, in his study, six hundred miles away.

'Robert, you must tell me honestly. Does Helen know about me?'

'Of course not, darling. I've told you that.'

'Yes, but how can I be sure? How can *you* be sure? Someone keeps telephoning me and putting the receiver down when I answer.'

'Look, sweetie, if Helen knew about you, I'd be the first to find out. She wouldn't keep quiet, I can promise you that. If you're worried by calls, tell the exchange. You can get nuisance calls monitored.'

'It hasn't reached that stage yet. It's annoying, that's all.'

Later on, I drew a deep bath and splashed into it the lemon and basil bath oil my sister had given me. It was fantastically expensive and the steam wafted deliciously. I lay back and closed my eyes. Alice returned to me. She would never have had the opportunity for such luxury. Had she smelt fishy and unwashed beneath the heavy skirts and coarse underwear? I imagined the muddy hems, the darned stockings, the stained underarms. The hands cracked with cold and dirt, the thin gold band of her wedding ring on a swollen chilblained finger. How hard it must have been. After bearing so many children her body would have become slackened and stretched,

her breasts drooping and veined. Had her young husband died here in the farmhouse? Had Alice? Was she
buried in the churchyard? Had they bumped her coffin
down the steep stairs where we had manhandled my
furniture? Had her six frightened, orphaned children
sobbed on the landing? Oh Alice, I mourned for your
short, hard life.

That was the night I was first woken from sleep by a
terrible seizure of fear. Somewhere in the velvet black-
ness, something had moved. I lay, terror thumping the
blood into my ears, straining for the sound which had
woken me. Very clearly, from downstairs I heard the
sound of the latch on the front door being lifted and
dropped. Too frightened to move, certainly unable to
reach for the light or the telephone, I lay waiting for
worse. Why hadn't Pilgrim barked? My alarm clock
ticked obliviously; the other thumping was my heart.
My ears buzzed with the thrumming silence.

Eventually the fear ebbed a little and I was able to put
on the light. Had I dreamed it? Were my going-to-bed
thoughts disturbing the present? Getting cautiously out
of bed, and holding the lamp as a makeshift truncheon,
I went to the top of the stairs and turned on the lights of
the stairwell. No sound. Nothing. I had frightened
myself nearly witless. Until dawn broke I lay in bed
with the lamp still switched on. As the weak grey,
end-of-year light seeped into the sky, I heard the sound
of the shepherd's quad bike as he came up the lane and
turned into the farm track. He was whistling. I was safe.

I went downstairs. Pilgrim hadn't moved from where
I'd tucked him up the night before. I made tea and
started to get dressed. My face looked pale and haggard
in the mirror

I still thought about Helen much of the time. One day,
for instance, I was standing behind a woman who could
have been Helen in the queue at Waitrose. She was

slim, tall, well-groomed, fiftyish. She wore a knee-length grey skirt, black tights and flat loafers, and her grey hair was cut short in a ragged modern style. She looked very, very attractive. Her trolley was full of expensive organic food. She was not wearing a wedding ring. This was the sort of woman Robert loved. She made me feel large, lumpish, unfinished. Amongst other things, my trolley contained a family-sized tub of pecan and toffee ice cream which I intended to eat, alone, in one glorious sitting. Shopping trolleys can be tremendously revealing. Mine, I feared, was not indicative of a together, well-balanced person. Defiantly I stopped on the way home at the fish and chip shop and bought a large cod and chips. Eaten out of the paper with plenty of salt, I enjoyed each greasy mouthful. Comfort eating, no doubt about it. The elegant shopper would at the same time have been picking at a grilled sardine and a green salad dressed with a little lemon juice. Well, good for her.

Now I knew Helen's name and her telephone number I was still no further finding out exactly where she lived, staking out her house and killing her. It was amazing how many cases there were in the papers at that time of mistresses killing wives, lovers, husbands, rivals. All of them were spectacularly unsuccessful. Often the killing was accomplished but this was followed very closely by arrest and then a pitiful display of remorse. The murder was the result of madness inspired by catatonic jealousy. Guns, knives, poison, cars . . . all these were used as weapons. No one had as yet beaten anyone to death with a loaf of wholewheat organic bread, but believe me, the possibility had crossed my mind.

When I was alone I contemplated these women who had led completely normal lives as far as I could tell. They worked variously as doctors' receptionists, in building societies, as hairdressers. One was a farmer's wife and was photographed laughing in a field with a cow. She had a large, unadorned sensible face. One was a primary-school headmistress of fifty-four. Their neighbours described them as quiet, pleasant, friendly women, always working for others, good wives and mothers. They had cooked meals, washed floors, ironed, caught buses, booked holidays, loved children and animals, married in hope and love, sat watching the television in the evenings; and they had all turned into killers. Could I become like them? Was it Helen I wanted to kill – or was it the way Helen made me feel about myself?

Robert's telephone calls were sometimes upsetting and unsatisfactory. Occasionally he sounded tired and did not want to talk much. He would terminate the conversation with, 'Well, I'd better go. Goodbye, sweetie.' He never lingered over endearments. Sometimes they seemed to me like duty calls, which he could tick off a list of things he had to get done. He would say, 'How are you?' but I could tell he didn't want a prolonged conversation and I often said, 'Oh, fine,' because I knew it was how he wanted it. Often our moods did not match. Sometimes I would ring him because I felt overpowered by love, caught perhaps by a memory of a precious time we'd had together, wanting to hear his voice just for a reassuring moment. Often it was at these times that he could not respond, sounding busy and distracted. If I minded and said I did, either then or afterwards, he would say, 'Don't be so unreasonable. I can't always talk to you, you know, just when it suits you. I don't ring you when you are working.' Which was perfectly true and reasonable.

Once he asked me if I was suffering from PMT. This made me crossest of all; as if I was a normally reasonable person acting in an uncharacteristic way. He refused to understand that all I wanted was to hear some pleasure in his voice, even if at the same time he was telling me that he couldn't talk to me. What I couldn't bear was his coldness; the switch on, switch off tap of his affection. After one of these conversations, I often took my coat from the peg behind the kitchen door and calling Pilgrim went for a walk. Stomping mechanically along the wet lanes at the dead end of the year, hands dug into my pockets, bent against the wind, the cold seemed to penetrate my head and clean out the misery and hurt. If I walked long enough, the open air and the exercise would lift my spirits. Sometimes when I got back home I would write him a note, usually saying I was sorry. Sometimes, but not often, I would find that he had telephoned me in my absence. His number was stored in my telephone's memory. I always wondered if he was the same with Helen. Did she depend on him as I did? Did he hurt her by this sudden coldness? I doubted it. He wouldn't dare. He didn't want to lose her.

Once he told me in a moment of reflection that he felt he sometimes treated me badly. I denied this vehemently, but afterwards I found that I was glad that he recognised that he did so, but then felt a great anxiety that I was turning into one of those women who get a kick out of being victims, doormats, just for the pleasure of the beater, the basher, the drunkard saying he is sorry in brief moments of remorse.

It would be wrong to suggest that our relationship was deteriorating at this time. I suppose it was moving on and changing in ways which did not always please or satisfy me, but it could also still be wonderful. I had one or two deliriously happy times in London when I seemed to have his full attention and devotion. One day we visited the Globe and spent a happy hour wandering round the exhibition before standing hand in hand like groundlings before the stage. It had begun to rain and I shivered. Robert looked at me tenderly and moved a wet strand of my hair. He kissed me gently on the forehead and held me to him with his chin resting on my head and both his arms round me. I felt a great surge of his love there in the place where so many tragedies and passions were acted out by players on the stage.

Not long afterwards I read a magazine article entitled *How To Know He's Cheating* which warned women of the signs that indicate a relationship is floundering. Kissing on the head, it said, should be reserved for children and dogs. It had no place in a mutually passionate relationship and should be treated with suspicion.

Chapter Nine

Toby was not going to let me off the hook regarding the village supper. He telephoned me a couple of evenings after our drinking spree, in that wasteland of days between Christmas and New Year, and arranged for a rehearsal. I repeated that I wasn't keen, that amateur performances were a mistake for a professional and that I was unhappy about playing with people of a doubtful standard. He told me I could play a solo. So I had to turn up at the village hall on a wind- and rain-soaked night, with a bundle of sheet music and my violin case. Toby was already there, turning on lights and organising a couple of other people I didn't recognise. A teenage girl was standing on the dusty stage with her arms crossed across her chest, rubbing her elbows. She looked miserable and had clearly been pressganged, as I had.

'Right!' said Toby cheerfully, springing up onto the stage and opening the lid on the piano. 'Thanks a lot for turning out on this awful night. Where's Ned? He said he'd come.'

'Not here yet,' observed a middle-aged woman, unnecessarily. She had a pleasant open face and was still wearing a woolly hat against the cold. She smiled a welcome at me.

'Well, let's start anyway,' Toby said. 'As you know, this isn't a concert as such, but just an entertainment for perhaps thirty minutes after dinner is finished and while people are still sitting at their tables. After that there'll be disco music for the younger ones and most of the oldies will leave, I should imagine. Now, we're really lucky in the village to have Jenny Johnson, who is a singer . . .' the middle-aged woman bobbed her head '. . . and Harriet Lennox who is a professional violinist.' I had to smile and acknowledge this introduction. 'Caroline is going to play the flute,' the teenager squirmed in anguish, 'and I'm going to bang the joanna. Ned is bringing his keyboard, Lester is going to play the trumpet, and I think that will be quite enough. Now can we just try and sort out a programme?'

Jenny had clearly come with a strong idea of what she was prepared to do and said so. Toby tactfully reduced her items to four and they had a run-through, with him accompanying her, really quite proficiently, on the piano. Her soprano voice resounded round the rafters, and she had sensibly chosen well-known songs from recent shows which most people would recognise. Caroline shyly said she could only play two pieces which she was preparing for her A-Level Music exam. One was a pretty lilting French melody and the other a folk song arranged by Arnold. I offered to accompany her and we had a run-through, which went reasonably well although she was terribly nervous. When she discovered that I was a teacher she relaxed a bit, as if she was in safe hands.

'This will be useful practice for you,' I said. 'You'll be doing your performance for your exam soon, won't you?'

'Yes, later on this term,' she whispered.

'Now Harriet, we can't let you off so lightly. What else will you do for us?'

'How about some folk songs, like I played you the other night?' I played them one which has a lovely haunting melody. It was called 'The Lonely Shepherdess' which I thought was most suitable. The others clapped when I'd finished and I took a mock bow.

By now, Ned had arrived, banging through the door while I was playing, in a gust of cold wind. I recognised him at once as the man I saw most mornings running past the farm. He was memorable because he took this morning exercise accompanied by a collie dog and pushing a little girl in a pushchair. I had often waved and smiled at them as they passed and had wondered who he was.

Ned was tall and thin with floppy brown hair. He looked unkempt tonight, in a baggy woolly jumper and jeans. He had the habit of running his hand back through his hair and making it stand on end. He clearly did not have a place of employment and I'd imagined him as a writer or an artist, definitely someone who worked from home.

'Sorry,' he said. 'I had to wait till Nicky got back from work. We didn't have a baby-sitter. That was lovely,' he said to me. 'I'm sorry I barged in and missed the first bit.'

'Thanks,' I said. We smiled at each other and I liked him instantly.

After a bit more discussion about the keyboard and the trumpet, Toby got out a notepad and wrote down the order of the pieces. I suggested that I play as people arrived, to break the ice and create a bit more atmosphere. 'People won't hear properly though,' objected Toby. 'You know there'll be a great hubbub of finding places and so on.'

'That doesn't matter,' I said. 'It's not a concert, as you pointed out.'

Soon after this we decamped to the pub. Caroline had an apple juice and sat in the corner looking as if she wanted to die. Toby was going to give her a lift home. I slid onto the bench next to her, but attempts at conversation merely intensified her agony. Ned sat opposite us.

'Where do you live?' he asked, sinking his face into a pint of Badger beer.

'Jerusalem Farm. You run past most mornings. I often wave at your little entourage!'

He laughed. 'Oh yes. Killing three birds with one stone. Keeps me fit, walks the dog and entertains Dido. I recognise you now. I'm usually so exhausted after getting up your hill that I'm speechless, or I'd say, "Good morning, madam!" Pushing the buggy must increase the aerobic effort considerably. You've got a greyhound, haven't you?'

'Yes, that's right. A rescued one.'

'What do you do?'

'I'm a boring old teacher, I'm afraid. I teach in Salisbury. What about you?' I pushed over my packet of crisps and he took a handful.

'I'm a peddler of electronic music – backing tapes, that sort of thing. I'm not actually a musician, more a technician. I work from home – I've got a studio in the cottage. I live in the valley below you . . . Mill Cottage.'

'What about Nicky?'

'She's a physiotherapist. Only works three days a week because of Dido. When she's working I take over . . .'

We were interrupted at this point and I was left thinking of this admirable arrangement. How well some husbands and wives seemed to manage their lives.

After some general chat about another rehearsal, Toby stood up and said, 'Come on, Caroline, or I'll have your mother after me.' I slid off the bench to let her out and we all said our goodnights.

As Toby helped Jenny on with her coat he said to me, 'How about tomorrow night for a drink? I'll give you a ring.'

'Great!' I said. Ned stood up and it looked as if this was the moment for us all to leave. We trooped out together and made a run across the car park, heads down, battling against the wind and rain.

What a nice man Ned is, I thought as I started the car. Attractive, too. And, of course, unavailable.

While I was still on holiday I thought I would drive into Bath and do some sale shopping. I was going to Poppy's for New Year's Eve and felt I would like something new to wear. I hadn't bought anything new for ages and Poppy's friends would all be London smart. I trawled round the usual High Street shops, uninspired by the cluttered rails of the garments nobody had wanted to buy. Eventually I found a smart shift dress in my size and fought my way into a communal dressing room. It was packed with young bodies in various stages of undress. Most had long, clean limbs and flat stomachs. The larger of us were lurking round the edges of the room, struggling to put dresses on over trousers, to reveal as little of ourselves as was possible.

Finding a secluded corner, I thought, Dammit and, unabashed, pulled off my jeans and sweater and catching sight of my underwear, resolved to go to M&S and treat myself to a new set. Robert always seemed oblivious to the allure of sexy underwear, simply wanting to get it off as quickly as possible, whereas I rather love knowing that underneath my outer layers is something exotic and slippery and terrifically sexy. In a way I was glad that he wasn't one of those men who buy hideous black nylon stuff with see-through bits and open crotches in which to truss their wives or girlfriends. I was thinking this as I struggled with the dress. It was far too small. I could only yank the zip halfway up. I checked the label – yes, it was a 14. Perhaps the sizing was wrong. I wrenched it off and had to go all through the performance of redressing in order to go back out into the store to find a sales assistant.

'Yeah, that's a fourteen,' she said. 'Do you need a sixteen?'

'No, I bloody don't,' I said. Nevertheless I tried the same dress in a larger size and even that was a close thing. It was a depressing exercise. There is nothing more disheartening than this struggle to get into clothes which are too small. Thirty-two and size 16. This was not a cheering thought. Around me were the twiglet girls of fourteen upwards, with skinny chests and no hips, slipping in and out of the clothes which were designed for their androgynous bodies. Here was I, the Rubens bather. Oh, sod it! I supposed that the time had come to acknowledge that I had reached a different stage of life. Apart from one middle-aged woman watching me from the other side of the room, and even she was skinny, there were very few girls over eighteen or size 10 in the place. I caught the woman's eye and smiled conspiratorially, but she looked hastily away.

I left the dress and walked out. Obviously, the more or less permanent state of dieting that I had fallen into recently was not a success. I thought about what I was going to eat every single morning and fantasised about being slim. Each day I resolved to pay for my indulgences with a strict and controlled regime which would remove the extra weight in a week or two. It could be done: I'd done it before. However, recently I had failed every time. I often managed to get through the day but by the evening I was ransacking the cupboards – especially when I was waiting for Robert to ring.

I envied those girls who gave up food when crossed in love. It seemed to me that I used it as an anaesthetic. It was worst in the evenings when I would graze until bedtime, and then go to bed feeling self-indulgent, weak-willed, greedy, disgusting. The lardy pounds were evidence. My bras cut into my flesh and my breasts spilled out of the cups. My knickers felt back to front, my trouser zips slid down and waistbands strained and chafed. I had to do skirts up with safety pins. I was growing larger by the day. I felt furious with Robert and

Helen. It was all their fault! Remarks made to me as a fat child came to the surface. Boys' taunts, nicknames. The Rubens bloody bather. I was sure that Helen was small and slim. I felt large, hulking and unlovable. No wonder Robert preferred her.

I drove home from Bath in a state of misery and close to tears. As soon as I got in I searched about for one of those self-improvement articles that always appear in the newspapers between Christmas and New Year. I had cut it out and resolved at the time to follow the worthy exhortations to cleanse my system, improve my complexion, do stretching exercises and learn a foreign language. That sort of thing. When I eventually found it, the diet recommended was based on cabbage soup, which one could fill up on, like a tanker. Stiffened with resolve, I made a large saucepanful of sludge. I would succeed. I would *not* allow Helen to triumph! My complexion would glow, as promised. My eyes would be bright and sparkling. I would be toned and honed for the New Year. Ready for combat.

The vegetable soup made me fart mightily, making Pilgrim jump and look round in alarm. As I ran my bath that evening I laid my jeans out on the floor. They looked huge, flattened out like that. Big enough for a large builder.

Poppy's New Year's Eve party kicked off in the new house into which she and Chris had recently moved. It was round the corner from where they had lived before, but located more firmly within the regenerated area of Shepherd's Bush. It was a five-bedroomed Georgian doll's house on four floors, each room perfectly proportioned.

Poppy now had a proper nanny, who came in daily, and a Filipino cleaner. She was looking wonderful, subtly expensive without abandoning her own eccentric, eclectic style. Her hair was washed twice a week at a very smart hairdresser and it tumbled down her back in glossy curls.

'God, Hazzy,' she said when she saw me, 'what are you wearing? Why are you in that great tent? You aren't pregnant, are you? Or in calf or something?'

She caught a glimpse of my stricken face and put her arms round me. I had had a miserable time getting ready, choosing something to wear that did not emphasise my figure, and thought I had been quite successful in the end, in a loose top and wide-legged trousers.

'Oops, sorry! But what are friends for, except to be brutally honest? It's just that it's not flattering. You need to make the most of what you've got. Flaunt it. Here, open some buttons and show off your enormous cleavage. You might as well use it to advantage, being so – well, gorgeously big. Chris will adore you like that. He's always complaining about my titlessness. Here, have a drink . . .' She passed me a glass of champagne. All about her on the scrubbed oak table in her terracotta kitchen were boxes and bags from an interior design, foodie shop.

'Look, we're starting here with champagne and bits to eat which I can just about manage because I bought them all, ha, ha, but I've still got to put them on plates and you know the drama that entails with me. Then we're going out to dins – about twenty of us. Is that all right?' I looked slightly alarmed, knowing I hadn't got much money to spare. 'Chris will pay for you – no, Christmas treat, so don't argue. Then I'll creep back here to bed, while all you unencumbered lot can dance the night away. My dear ma is babysitting and she doesn't want to be too late.'

She looked at me shrewdly. 'Come upstairs – I've got a skirt you can wear. No, it's elastic-waisted . . . all floaty and delicious. Those ghastly things you've got on are going in the bin. Great elephant-bottom trousers don't suit anybody. I won't allow you to send them to a

104

charity shop for some refugee who has already suffered quite enough. I can't bear watching the News when you see the poor victims of some Third World disaster standing about looking dejected in the rubble of their homes wearing the most awful polyester skirts and golfing jumpers airlifted in by Oxfam. I mean, natural catastrophes are bad enough without having to suffer somebody else's shopping mistakes.'

Having destroyed any confidence I might have had, Poppy forced me into her skirt and found me a beautiful shirt and adorned me with her jewellery. She was right, I did look much better.

'You're still wonderfully pretty,' she said kindly, 'with your milkmaid's complexion, corn-coloured hair and goddess-like abundance.' Now I live in the country all Poppy's descriptions of me are bucolic. She was trying to make up for telling me I looked a disaster.

Jessica came in to fiddle about with her mother's make-up and I hugged her. She had grown and her once plump little body felt skinny and frail. Her knees were little knobs on her stick-like legs. She put her small hands on either side of my face and kissed me. We smiled at each other. 'I saw snogging on the television,' she said. 'It was really pooh.'

The party turned out to be mostly new friends of Poppy and Chris. The old orchestra crowd seemed to have faded out of Poppy's life and I could understand why. Her current lifestyle was so different that there would be little point of reference and she hadn't played professionally for some years. Her new friends were smart and super cool. The men, and quite a few of the women, had City jobs and huge salaries, I guessed. They talked a lot about bonuses.

Two of the wives were interior designers. One was writing a book on curtains and one owned a children's continental clothes shop. There was a lot of shrieking amongst the women as they identified designer labels on one another and complained in a competitive way about exhaustion. Some of them were married. Some, like Poppy, had children and nannies. This section clearly found the subject of childcare riveting. They were all thin. They all had sharp hairstyles. I loomed amongst them, feeling large and thatched. Thank goodness for dear Chris who hugged me, gazed admiringly at my breasts and said how nice it was to feel a real woman.

Because I didn't know anybody I found myself filling a maiden aunt sort of role and being tremendously helpful in the kitchen and passing the bits of sushi and stuff round. From the way I was ignored, I realised that those who had not been introduced to me thought I was the caterer. Poppy did her best, dragging me about and saying, 'You must meet my dearest, oldest friend . . .' and I was then subjected to a top-to-toe scrutiny and an expression of the merest polite interest. I knew what the trouble was. I was not someone anyone wanted to know. Being a teacher, of course, was beyond the pale. I certainly wasn't someone useful to the network. I tried to smile brightly and say something witty about the food I shoved under their noses. The women refused to eat more than two canapés whereas the men were greedy and helped themselves to two at a time, cramming them in their mouths without stopping talking.

In the end, I got fed up and went and talked to Poppy's mother who was putting the children to bed. Tom was already asleep; Jess was in the bath. I showed her how to do soap bubbles and we had fun, chortling and splashing. She was sitting on my lap wrapped in a towel when a man came upstairs, looking for the loo. I had noticed him being helpful with the refilling of glasses. He was rather short and plump with glasses. The male equivalent of me, I suppose, in terms of attractiveness.

He looked in the bathroom door and said, 'Hi!' I introduced Poppy's mother and he came in and shook hands. He had good manners. He told me there was a general movement downstairs and suggested that I came down and joined the group leaving to walk round the corner to the Italian restaurant. He reminded me that his name was Mike and that he was a lawyer. He followed me down the stairs and when I saw Poppy's face at the bottom, looking up at us, I realised that he was destined for me. I narrowed my eyes at her and made a sucking-lemon face.

In actual fact, beggars can't be choosers and all that, Mike was good company and I liked him more than most of the others. He was noisy and cheerful, but also a good listener and seemed interested in my life in a genuine way. We got on well which was a good thing because the bloke on the other side of me at the table actually sat with his back slightly turned on me, totally taken up with the girl on his left. She was as thin as a whippet in a minuscule dress and very loud. As she got more and more drunk she became more and more foul-mouthed. When she got up to go to the Ladies she tripped and stumbled in her vast heels, said, 'Fuck!' loudly and teetered off. Mike and I grimaced. 'She's a barrister,' he said.

Everyone was drinking very fast and the harassed waiters set down more bottles the length of the table and whisked away the empties. Poppy was flirting with an Italian banker at one end of the table. He clearly had his hand up her skirt. Chris, at the other end, was sitting with his arm round a pretty girl with jet-black hair and a white face. I tried really hard to find it fun but it was an uphill struggle. I felt flat and dull but managed to smile and pretend it was all entertaining. I wished I was at home, holed up in the cottage, listening to the owls.

We stood up for the stroke of midnight and made a ragged cross-handed circle to sing 'Auld Lang Syne'. The

107

man on my left didn't bother to join hands with me but preferred to clasp the buttocks of the drunk barrister instead. Her tiny skirt rode up and you could see her knickers. After all the cheering and Happy New Yearing and silly kissing there was a general sort-out and Poppy said she would have to go home and Chris came and put his arm round her and the Italian moved off. Mike asked me if I wanted to go on to a club and I said, 'Okay,' and we trooped out into the gaudy night. We shared a taxi with some of the others. He tried to kiss me on the back seat and bit my neck, and I knew it was all a depressing mistake, for him too.

'Look,' I said, struggling to sit up. 'I'm actually in a relationship.'

He surfaced and removed his glasses. 'Poppy said you weren't,' he said, wiping them on his handkerchief. He looked younger and more vulnerable without his specs.

'Well, I am.'

'Fair enough.'

After that he seemed quite relieved – as if he'd done his duty and been let off the hook. I imagined Poppy geeing him up, saying that I would be ideal for him. We went to a club, got on really well and had fun. Mike was a hopeless and embarrassing dancer, but that didn't matter because he was unselfconscious and it was New Year's Eve. There were people falling over everywhere. Finally we walked back to Poppy's together, taxis being unobtainable, and the streets were full of revellers. I invited him down to Jerusalem Farm for a weekend. He immediately said, 'Great. When?' so I knew he had as many gaps to fill in his life as I did. He took my telephone number outside Poppy's front door and kissed me goodnight. It was a relief not to have to go through the 'Come in for a coffee' routine.

I only had a few hours' sleep and got up the next morning feeling, as usual for New Year's Day, terrible. I ate an enormous toast and Marmite breakfast, helped

Poppy clear up, took Jess for a walk and then drove home on wonderfully empty roads. It was a grey day and the great rolling Downs were as grey as the sky, with the long grass bleached by winter. I liked its bleakness and openness. I enjoyed being alone with the day in front of me to fill as I wished. I was okay. I was in charge. I was going to get my eating under control. I was moving on, letting go, whatever the jargon is which covers this kind of emotional journey. I collected Pilgrim from my mother, who had spent New Year's Eve with some neighbours.

'I'm having a few people to drinks tomorrow evening, darling – only about a dozen. Do you think you could come? I'd like you to meet them.'

'Yes, Ma. Sure, I'd love to. I'll come and help with the butlering.' She is such a wily old crone that even then I had no idea what she was up to.

Chapter Ten

When I got back to the farm that day, my head was beginning to pound and I was starting to feel the need to stuff myself with carbohydrates to soak up the drink of the night before. However, my mind was taken off this because there was a trailer and one of those armoured personnel carriers favoured by people in the country parked outside the cottage. I got out of my car and found Toby in the garden driving in some fence-posts and nailing up some wire netting. He looked healthy and pink-cheeked. I kissed him and he put his arm round me.

'Happy New Year,' he said, giving me a hug. 'Here you are. Sheep. They'll chomp their way through all this rubbish in your garden. I can see you are not going to take up lawn-mowing. I'm fencing off this bit round the house in case you want to grow some flowers or stuff. There's masses of room for them where the old orchard was.'

'Toby,' I said, 'you are a star. How exciting! I really will be The Lonely Shepherdess.' I peered over the back of the trailer. Inside were four brown-and-white lady sheep and a curly-horned brown-all-over one who looked masculine. 'Four lady sheep and a man?' I asked.

'God!' said Toby. 'Four ewes and a ram – do at least get that right! They belong to my mother but she can

111

spare them. The ewes are due to lamb in May. Pedro, the ram, is in charge. They'll look after themselves. If the weather turns, I'll come by and throw them some hay. Their feet have been done and they are properly wormed et cetera so they are absolutely maintenance free, except you will have to fill up this trough with water. Have you got a hose? Well, get one. Until then, buckets will do.' He slammed in the last post and tacked on the wire. 'There. That should be sheep-proof.'

Together we unloaded the sheep and with the help of a bucket of nuts Toby had in the back of his vehicle, we tempted them into their new corral. Immediately they set about eating, their jaws working in a side-to-side motion. Pilgrim looked at them with great interest.

'Will he savage them, or worry them or whatever the term is?' I asked.

'Very unlikely. If he shows too much interest, put him in with them. Pedro will sort him out in about five minutes flat. He's not the slightest bit alarmed by dogs.'

'They've got eyes like boiled sweets – like humbugs. They are *so* pretty. Toby, I'm really excited. Thank you so much. Will they really do the gardening for me?'

'Absolutely,' said Toby, wiping his hands on his corduroy bottom. 'Now can I have a coffee?'

'Sure,' I said. 'You deserve more than that.'

I unlocked the kitchen door and felt a real rush of pleasure at being home. The stove was still alight and the cottage felt quite warm for once. Toby shot some coke onto the fire while I boiled the kettle and told him about Poppy's party. He had been to a dinner party, which he said was a bit 'coupley'. Some poor spare girl had been asked for him. I told him I knew what he meant. 'Everyone else was married with children,' he told me. 'It shouldn't create such a chasm between us but it does. I find the women worst. They sort of write you off if you can't join in the "How old are yours?" talk. They all seem completely obsessed by child-rearing.'

112

'Was the girl nice?' I asked. 'The one intended for you?'

'Yeah. She was fine – perfectly okay.'

'I met a perfectly okay man, too. Poppy had him lined up for me.'

'Perfectly okay is exactly what it says though, isn't it? I don't suppose I'll make the effort to see her again. I didn't take her number or anything.'

'I did more than that. I've invited Mike to come and stay. I really liked him, but that's all. He was good company and good fun. I expect Poppy is disappointed that we're not engaged already.' Toby laughed. I realised that I felt extremely happy, drinking coffee with him in my pretty kitchen, Pilgrim curled up in his bed by the stove and my sheep outside the door. I was glad that I registered it as happiness. It wasn't a significant moment but out of it grew a contentment I hadn't experienced for a long time. My life seemed, at that moment, good exactly as it was.

My mother's party the next day entailed my driving over to her cottage in the early evening to give her a hand to get things ready. She had already lit the fire in her beamed drawing room and drawn the curtains. Her lamps glowed and her little arrangements of holly and Christmas roses and sweet winter jasmine, which she had set amongst candles on various tables, made the pretty room look festive and cheerful. Ma was wearing a soft, pale blue sweater and a neat dark skirt. She had on her diamond clip earrings which sparkled and made her face look really quite young and pretty.

I am much larger than her and when I kissed her she felt frail in my arms. I suddenly felt sentimental. I wanted her to be there for ever. Never one for displays of emotion, she disentangled herself and moved smoothly off into the kitchen and got me laying transparent slivers of smoked salmon onto brown bread slices. I then had to trim off the crusts and quarter the slice and arrange the pieces attractively, decorating the plate with parsley and scoops of shiny black lumpfish caviar. Considering I play a delicate instrument with some precision I am clumsy and cack-handed. I could sense my mother anxiously over-seeing my efforts as she piped the filling into scooped-out halves of quails' eggs. Home-made cheese straws were warming in the oven, together with tiny quiches.

'Lovely stuff, Ma. You are clever.' I finished my salmon job and watched my mother tidying and rearranging the plates. I ate the crusts I'd cut off. God, I am hopeless, I thought cheerfully. My mother had got bottles of a good Spanish Cava chilling in the fridge and I put six bottles on a tray and promised that I would do the opening and pouring the moment people arrived.

'Douglas will help,' she said. 'He's good at that sort of thing.'

'Douglas?'

'Douglas Croxford. I don't think you've met him. He moved into the village last year. Retired RN.'

'Married?'

'Widower. Rather hard on him, I think. He is a good coper in the practical sense but lonely. Finds village life a bit claustrophobic.'

'Can't you pair him off with one of your old girls?' Ma laughed shortly and put on her oven gloves to get something out of the oven.

Her guests arrived promptly at six o'clock and I was kept busy handing round glasses. 'Oh! How lovely!' 'What a treat . . . thank you so much.' How polite and gracious were these elderly people. Silver hair (and variations of slightly pink, mauve and blue) bobbed and nodded, well-set and sprayed into place. Faces were well-powdered and lipsticked. The men were dapper with polished shoes and clean fingernails, pinkly newly shaved with matching ties and handkerchiefs. They listened to one another with interest, asked appropriate

114

questions, passed round plates, introduced others – the social manoeuvres all effortless and graceful. I thought of Poppy's party – the loud boastfulness, the selfishness, the lack of social grace. My mother's generation had much better manners. They were well-informed from hours of Radio 4 and reading broadsheets from cover to cover. Perhaps there was a little too much emphasis on the successes of children and grandchildren.

'Yes, I have two grandsons . . . both such bright boys. My daughter, of course, was at Oxford. That's where she met Nick, her husband.'

'My son is in London. He has three children. Oh, what a life they lead! Cottage in Suffolk, skiing, holidays in Kenya. Now did you say you were married? Never mind, my dear, you are still very young, and of course things are so different now. Girls don't rush into marriage like we did.'

I had variations of this conversation most of the evening, but not from Douglas who was rather gruff and monosyllabic. I wondered why he came to this sort of party, and had a vision of his neat, ship-shape house, empty and lifeless apart from the ticking of clocks and the murmur of the refrigerator. Loneliness, I suppose, forced him out to stand tall and silent in the corners of these gatherings, while women chirruped round him.

Pilgrim, stretched out on the hearth rug, was a great success. He lapped up the attention and was passed occasional tit-bits.

Douglas soon relieved me of the refuelling duty. He was tall, in pretty good shape, with a long intelligent face. The noise grew. The slightly deaf were talked to loudly and clearly. 'No, I didn't manage the service this morning. I have a bit of a leg, you know.' There were jokes, affectionate teasing, laughter. And then everyone began to leave. It would have been impolite to linger. Douglas hovered about helping to collect glasses on trays. The three of us shared the leftover salmon, standing up in the kitchen. My mother poured us more wine. She drinks very little and she was flushed and elated by the success of her party.

'Sorry, Ma, no more for me. I'm driving. It's been a really good party.'

'Dull for you, darling. All us old things. Thank you for coming and being such a help.'

'It was fun. I enjoyed it.'

Douglas had put on a navy overcoat and was preparing to leave.

'Oh Douglas! Don't go. I've some soup to warm. Stay and eat.'

After a bit of mild protesting about being a nuisance, he removed his overcoat again.

'Ma, I *must* go. I've got a rehearsal at nine o'clock.' I called Pilgrim, who got up from the fire with great reluctance. My mother followed me out without a coat, down her little garden path to where my car was parked on the lane.

'Harriet, there's something I must tell you.'

I stopped, my hand on the door of my car, checked by the tone of her voice. A lump of dread caught in my throat. Was she going to tell me she was ill . . . going to die?

'Douglas has asked me to marry him and I've accepted. Darling, don't look so shocked. We are both so happy.'

I drove home with my thoughts in turmoil. I had managed to go through the motions, kissed her warm, soft cheek, said, 'Ma!! How amazing! How brilliant!' and went back inside with her to kiss Douglas who was standing looking anxious with a tea towel in his hand. He made a lot of harrumping noises and reached for my mother's hand.

'Look,' I burbled on, 'it's wonderful. I'm sure you'll be very happy. I don't know you – but I'm sure you will. I'm sorry I've got to go, but I do *have* to. Although I suppose, three's a crowd in your case. Mum, you are a dark horse.'

'All right, darling,' said my mother, calmly. 'Do go, or you'll be late.'

I couldn't believe it. My mother getting married. Sharing her kitchen, her bathroom, her bedroom with a man. I thought of her in her underwear – naked, even – with a man. It was impossible. I realised now that she looked in love. Still calm and unemotional but lit up, warmed by Douglas's affection and attention. Oh God! I knew I was jealous. Jealous of my mother. Jealous because she had found someone to make her happy, and jealous of Douglas. I needed my mother as she was. I didn't want to share her with a stranger. How could she do it to me? How could she? I felt angry and hurt, and ashamed because I recognised the baseness of my nature.

This was not the line I took when she and I met later in the week. I'd discussed it with Poppy. Predictably she told me I was selfish and shortsighted, that my mother had been alone for fifteen years and was hardly rushing into remarriage. She said that she deserved my support. I sat staring at the wall, telephone in hand.

'Poppy, I know all this, but it doesn't alter how I actually *feel*, which is pissed off. I know I shouldn't, but I feel betrayed by her, as if she and Douglas have conspired against me.'

'You'll get over it. If you got yourself a life, my dear, you'd soon have this in perspective.' Poppy was always honest and usually right.

As it was I now faced my mother across a wobbly pub table, with a basket of packet butters between us. 'Ma, are you sure? I mean, you are so settled, so organised. You have your own routine, your own way of doing things. Are you sure you want to share your home with someone, to give up your independence, to compromise?'

117

'Darling, I'm longing to. Douglas is a good and a kind man. It will be wonderful to have someone to share things with. It's not a question of giving things up, or losing anything . . . it's a case of increasing enjoyment of life because there's someone to share it with.'

'But are you sure? You manage so well on your own. I thought you really rather enjoyed it.'

My mother shrugged. 'It was the card I was dealt, and so I got on with it: I had no other option. Up until now I haven't been tempted or given the opportunity to change it. Now I have. I don't think being solitary is a natural state. Sorry, Harriet, this is not directed at you. You are young with your life in front of you,' I snorted derisively, 'and I'm old and look forward to sharing the rest of my life with a man I've become very fond of. Life on one's own can be really very desolate when one's getting on in years. I'm tired of standing in front of joints in the butcher's and thinking, It's not worth cooking that just for me. And there are so many other things like that – not bothering to light the fire if one's alone, going to bed early, because sitting reading on one's own is so miserable, not taking holidays, not having a weekend lunch in a pub. It may sound like a trivial list, but what I'm trying to say is that the quality of one's life seems reduced on one's own. I want a companion. Surely you understand?'

'Yes, I do. But none of those things are worth it if you're not sure you want to share them with Douglas. I don't know how you can be so sure.'

'Believe me, I can.'

'Well, here's to you both!' and I raised my glass. Truthfully I was happy for her, but I still felt miserable.

Robert failed to understand.

'It's just taken you by surprise,' he said. 'You'll get used to it. He's a nice man, you say? Well then, what's the problem?'

'Me – I'm the problem. It seems an unnatural order of events to have one's mother married off while lumpen thirty-something daughter lurks on the shelf.'

'Don't be ridiculous. You can't see yourself like that. Someone like you could easily get married if you wanted to. Singledom is your choice. Why don't you accept that?'

Why did my friends turn my mother's intended marriage into an attack on me? Couldn't they see I needed sympathy?

Chapter Eleven

The evening of the village feast arrived. I did not set out with much enthusiasm. In fact, I found myself reluctant to go at all and even toyed with the idea of bunking off and saying that I was ill. However, loyalty to Toby and anxiety about Caroline made me resolve to go through with it.

I was so used to doing things in the evening with a load of friends, or meeting up with them first in a pub before going to a party, that I found setting off on my own surprisingly daunting. I couldn't decide what to wear. Toby had been vague about the dress code and I spent a dispiriting half an hour trying things on and then discarding them in a pile on my bedroom floor. I had managed to lose a little bit of weight since New Year. Just a few days of restrained eating had had a noticeable effect, so at least I could jam myself into all my clothes. In the end I settled on a long stretchy skirt and a satin shirt in a lovely electric-blue shade. At any rate, I would be comfortable when I was playing.

I washed my hair, put on some make-up and squirted myself with a delicious Jo Malone scent my sister had given me. It had been a gift from a grateful client but Isabel is one of those women who wear the same signature scent all their lives. Suddenly I thought of Alice Frost, the young widow with six children, who had inhabited this house in 1891. Four years later, she was dead. I don't know why she so abruptly occupied my mind. I froze, sensing her presence in the room with me as the perfume hung about us. Alice, I was certain, was standing just behind me. Had she ever had the privilege of enjoying clothes, of dabbing herself with lavender water and going out for an evening? Were there village feasts when she had lived at Jerusalem Farm? Did she dance a lively reel to the music of a fiddle?

'Sorry, Alice,' I whispered. 'Sorry that I can life my life and that yours was so briefly over and so burdensome.' Then she was gone. The room was still and calm. There were no ghostly manifestations. But why had I suddenly thought of her under the mist of scent? Weird, these sensations I got. I couldn't explain them to anybody. They would have thought I was going mad.

It was a lovely cold clear night – the sort you can only appreciate in the countryside where the stars are undimmed by the sodium lights of cities. I spent a few moments gazing up at the brilliant sky after I had locked the door behind me, wishing I had someone to share it with, to say, 'Look! Look up at the stars!' Pilgrim barked from inside, protesting at being left. He was better off in his bed by the stove than in the cold car, but he didn't know it.

Toby and Ned were already there when I arrived at the hall. A busy team of ladies was setting tables and hurrying back and forth into the kitchen. Nobody took any notice of my entrance. There was a warm steamy smell of food cooking, and a retired colonel type was uncorking wine at a table set up with glasses and bottles by the door. Toby came over, dressed in a striped shirt and a tie with bright peacocks marching on it, and kissed me. Ned had smartened himself up too and was in a clean navy sweater and chinos with unexpected creases. He waved to me from where he was fiddling about with cables with two young men in black T-shirts and combat trousers who were setting up the disco. They both had daffodil-yellow hair tied into little scrunchy knots with elastic bands.

The colonel gave me a glass of wine to try: 'See what you think of this. Highly quaffable, I'd say!' and I put it on a window sill while I took off my coat and tuned my violin. I played a few bars and than ran through the whole of 'The Lonely Shepherdess'. The gang of workers clapped when I had finished and I took a swig of wine.

'That was charming,' said the military gentleman, who introduced himself as John Hopper from Green Lane. 'The violin is such a lovely instrument when it is played as well as you do.'

'Thank you,' I smiled back, I then strolled over to where Ned and Toby were moving tables.

'Hi,' said Ned. 'How are you doing? Careful, Toby, you'll leave no room for the waitresses.'

'Fine,' I replied. 'Can I do anything to help?'

'We're okay, thanks,' said Toby. 'Nearly done.'

'No baby-sitting problems?' I said to Ned, wanting to keep the conversation going.

He put down his end of the table and pushed his floppy hair back. 'No. Nicky's got Dido tonight.'

'But isn't she coming? Nicky, I mean?'

'No, she's not. She wasn't invited actually. She doesn't live here, you see. She lives near Frome.'

'Oh, right,' I said, utterly puzzled but not showing it. Was he separated, divorced? He wasn't going to enlighten me and I felt I couldn't ask any more leading questions. He was so easy and unaffected and I liked his smile which caused deep vertical furrows on either side of his mouth.

I downed another glass of wine and felt terrific. Caroline arrived, thinner and paler than ever in a dusty long black skirt with a trodden-down hem and a black tight-fitting top which emphasised her concave thin-ness. She looked unutterably miserable. I tried to cheer her up and ran through her two pieces, which she played quite well. Then I gave her a glass of wine off the colonel's table. She looked at it doubtfully.

'Go on,' I said gently. 'One glass won't hurt you. Helps your nerves.' She smiled wanly. She had intricate henna tattoos all over the back of her hands which looked large and knobbly on the end of her stick arms.

People were starting to arrive; the noise level swelled. The colonel was insisting everyone should have a glass of wine and he teased the timid ladies who asked for a soft drink. Elderly women in their best frocks came in in little gaggles and moved up the room to roost together in clusters. I recognised the shepherd and his wife whom I had never met. Where he was small, brown and wiry, she was large, white and floury-looking. He was very spruced up with slicked-down hair and a patterned sweater. He winked and waved at me.

The keeper arrived with his wife, who trained his Labradors; she gave him sharp barked orders to get her a drink and find her a seat away from the radiators. The lady vicar dashed in, smiling and important, ushering two very old girls with sticks to a table near the door from where one smiled and nodded and the other glowered and dribbled. Several couples with loud and confident voices walked in en masse and sorted out tables for themselves. They had come from The Manor, The Old Vicarage, The Mill House, The Hill House. The women stuck together in their London-influenced clothes while their men greeted other local men with whom they had done business. Although the divisions of money and power were unassailable, men who had cut their lawns, trimmed their hedges, and acted as their builders and roofers were clasped by the arm in a matey fashion.

I was so busy watching all this that for a while I did not notice Toby gesticulating for me to begin. Finding a space near the drinks table, I started off with a couple of jigs. People smiled encouragingly and talked all the louder. I played for about ten minutes until the room was full and a large gang of awkward, shoving young people arrived. They had been hanging round the doors, smoking, until the last moment. When I finished playing there was a lull and a few people clapped which encouraged others to join in. I bowed and moved back out of the limelight.

The vicar sprang forward, her face very pink and glistening, and suggested in her pulpit voice that carried over the din that everyone find a table because the ladies were ready in the kitchen and she was going to say Grace. She had on her dog collar and an unbecoming blue blouse tucked into an immense floral skirt. If women priests are to be taken seriously they have got to sort out their clothing, I thought. Such large bottoms, thus displayed, do not give rise to reverent thoughts.

Toby and Ned had saved me a place; Ned was waving across the room and pointing to the empty chair. I went to the Ladies which was outside in the cold courtyard and looked at my reflection in the brown spotted glass. My eyes were bright and I looked pretty and happy. As I made my way back across the room a few old people caught my arm and said, 'That was lovely, dear. You play ever so well.' The colonel tried to make me sit by him, getting his beaky-looking wife, Audrey, to move up. I caught her giving my grandmother's garnet necklace the once-over. I was duly assessed and categorised.

'Please don't move,' I said. 'Look, I've got a place saved for me there.' I just made it to Ned's side when the vicar, whose name I had learned was Pauline, started a long and soppy Grace about the joys of the countryside. The moment she had finished the kitchen ladies burst forth with trays of plates. The first course was pâté and French bread or soup. In no time at all, everyone was served and the wine strategically placed on the tables was passed and glasses filled. Toby was

125

terrifically good at seeing to other people, getting up to fetch water and find an old lady's handbag which had strayed under the table.

'Is that your bag or your leg, Doris?' he asked as he groped under the tablecloth.

'oooh! It's me leg, you naughty boy!'

Ned smiled across at me. 'Great playing,' he said.

'Thanks.' I beamed at him. 'The good thing about all my years of performing in crummy orchestras is that I'm not nervous any more. I can do this sort of thing without feeling sick.'

'Unlike poor Caroline.' Ned indicated Caroline sitting halfway down the room with her parents. Her mother wore a shirt with its collar turned up in that curious manner beloved of middle-class women, and was wearing a pair of tartan trousers with an important-looking belt boasting a grand buckle. Her father was large and meaty-looking. Sitting next to them, their daughter looked even frailer and more transparent than usual. Did they notice, I wondered, that she was fading away? How were they dealing with her agony? Exasperated and at their wits' end, I imagined. Caroline's pâté remained untouched and she pulled at the lump of bread, crumbling it into pieces.

'So how do you like living here?' asked Ned, and once again we drifted into easy conversation. I told him about my flight from London and my job, and even about my mother's forthcoming marriage. As I recounted the story of her drinks party and her announcement, my hurt feelings seemed to shrink to a manageable size. I could even laugh about it. 'So here I am at thirty-two, about to be a bridesmaid to my mother,' I joked.

Ned told me that he too had recently moved from London where he had had a half share in a recording studio in Golders Green. He had found Mill Cottage quite by accident and had fallen in love with it.

'I can lie in bed at night and hear the stream running along the back and it is the most wonderful and tranquil sound after years of police sirens and street noise. Electronic equipment is easily installed, and before too long I got an office up and running and found I could do my music just as effectively here as there. I go to London about once a month just to tout for work, although I'm glad to say that most of my important contacts know where to find me. It's been good for Nicky, too, to have me closer. She has needed quite a bit of support.'

I nodded. What was he talking about? Did divorced couples normally behave so reasonably to one another? It seemed unusual. I was just about to ask him about how long they had been apart when there was a flurry of activity and the waitresses were whisking away the first course and bringing on plates of beef stew and mushrooms with piles of mashed potato.

Pauline was on her feet and directing the men to move down the tables three to their right. Ned got up obediently and, smiling a farewell, moved with his glass to sit next to the lady from the Post Office. Her wiry brass helmet of hair was freshly welded into shape and she wore a peony-pink jumper bristling with black diamanté roses. A pleasant-looking man in his fifties came to take Ned's place. He was an accountant called Roger who worked in a large firm in Salisbury and lived in a modern house in a small new development behind Manor Farm. He was easy to talk to and asked politely about my work and life, and told me he loved walking the green lane behind Jerusalem Farm. He said it was thick with primroses in the spring.

On my other side was a young farmer who said his name was Geoffrey and that he was a friend of Toby's. He pointed out his pretty dark-haired wife who taught at the primary school. Geoffrey looked more like another accountant than a farmer, being rather weedy and pale with thinning hair. Only his hands looked red and chapped from outdoor work. He said that farming was disastrous and he didn't know how much longer they'd be able to hang on. Three days a week he worked on a market stall that toured the local towns – 'just to put food on the table,' he said. His anguish was so raw and unexpected that I could only murmur in sympathy about how awful it must be. 'The hardest part is having to live off Karen,' he said, glancing down the table to where she was flirting with a tall man in a checked shirt.

I poured him another glass of wine and said something fatuous about things getting better. My huge ignorance about life in the country, the real drama of BSE and milk quotas, of TB and sheep prices rendered me inadequate. All I could do was look and sound sympathetic. Geoffrey sighed and watched his wife whose face had a kind of hectic liveliness. Taking the conversational plunge I asked Geoffrey what music he liked and found that I could divert him by talking about a band he had played in when he was still at school.

Before too long Pauline was on her feet indicating another change. This time it was the ladies who had to move in the opposite direction. This caused a great deal of difficulty with bags and cardigans and spectacles. Sturdy legs and ankles in party shoes with unfamiliar heels climbed out of difficult corners where the chairs were close together. I found myself next to one of the rather grand men I had noticed at first. He was about forty, I judged, and very smooth and confident. He had swept-back blond hair and a handsome arrogant face just rounding at the chin with success and the good things of life. He scrutinised me closely.

'Hello,' he said, with the sort of emphasis that suggested I was the only woman he wanted to meet.

'Hi,' I replied.

He pushed his chair round so that he was half-turned towards me. 'Now where have you been hiding? You are not going to tell me that you live in the village?'

'Yup, I do. At Jerusalem Farm. What about you?'

'We live at Hill House. That's my wife, Lucinda, over there.' He pointed to a skinny blonde in a skimpy mini-dress with long hair and a lot of jewellery.

'What do you do?' I asked.

'Banker. I'm a weekly boarder. Only get down here Friday night – back Monday morning. Do you ride?'

'Ride what?'

He laughed. 'Not a bicycle. Horses?'

'No. Much too large and hairy with two frightening ends. Do you?'

'Yah. Most people do round here.'

'Oh.' I rather doubted this could be true, looking at the assembled company. 'What sort of riding do you do?' I couldn't imagine him trotting peacefully about the lanes.

'Team chase. Hunt. That sort of thing.'

'All fast and dangerous?'

'That's it!' he laughed and then added: 'You're not an anti, are you?'

'Anti Harriet to my sister's children. Yes, I am.'

He laughed again. 'Now tell me all about yourself, and tell me who you know. We must get you round for supper.'

I told him briefly and saw his ears prick up at the school bit. He must have daughters reaching that age group. Networking, connecting, was the name of the game. He had me labelled and filed in a few minutes. He also found me attractive. His lazy eyes moved up and down, stopping to rest quite openly on my breasts. A half-smile played round his lips. 'Now, why aren't you married?' he asked.

I smiled lazily back. 'Ah,' I said. 'That would be telling.'

Lucinda appeared behind him. Her bony little face was sharp and discontented. 'Jakers, don't have any more to drink, you old soak.' She turned to me. 'He's got to drive the baby-sitter home.'

He caught her hand. 'You must meet this wonderful girl,' he said. 'Darling, she teaches the violin.'

Lucinda looked me up and down. 'Really. How wonderful.' Her voice was flat with lack of interest.

At that point I abandoned him and went to collect my violin and tune it ready for the entertainment. Plates of lemon meringue pie were circulated, and platters of cheese plonked on the tables. The waitresses looked tired and harassed as they tried to move up and down the crowded, noisy room. At one end, the congregated old and deaf had given up the attempt to communicate and sat in companionable silence. One old man had gone to sleep. The younger and livelier tables had eaten and drunk well and there was a lot of raucous laughter. I began to think that Toby was much mistaken in his style of entertainment. It would have been better to get on with the dancing straight away. However, Jenny Johnson was already standing on the front of the stage waiting for the signal to begin. Ned had organised the lights to dim and a spotlight to play on her. She took up the classic singer's pose and smiled brightly at the room.

Realising that something was about to begin, people started to shush one another. I could see Pauline standing by the stage, preparing another announcement, moving her arms and shoulders about as if getting up steam, a self-important look on her face. Toby short-circuited her by playing some crashing chords on the piano, and Jenny launched forth, her confident, powerful style carrying her audience with her. The songs she had chosen were so well-known that people hummed and mouthed the words. I relaxed. It was going to be okay.

It was my turn next and there were wolf whistles when I went into the spotlight. Some male voice at the back shouted, 'Get them off!' This was followed by disapproving noises and laughter. I galloped through my two gigs and a hornpipe and finished with the haunting 'Lonely Shepherdess'. When I finished I gave a quick half-bow and caught Jake's eye. He was clapping in an exaggerated way. I got off the stage and went to look for Caroline. There was no sign of her. Eventually I found her in the Ladies. From the nail-varnishy smell and her ashen face she had clearly been sick.

'Oh Caroline,' I said. She looked into my face, distraught. I put my arms round her little bird-like shoulders. 'Oh my dear, you must get help. You *must*.'

Her tiny frame was wracked by a sudden convulsion of sobs. She clung to me like someone drowning. 'I can't, I can't, *I can't*!' she wailed.

Much later I put her into my car and went back into the hall. People were already beginning to leave. The disco had started and the throbbing music and flashing lights transformed the room. The tables had been cleared and pushed back. Some of the elderly, determined to get their money's worth sat on, washed up round the edges as if by a tide. The floor was taken by leaping dancers. I saw Geoffrey's wife dancing in an extrovert way with Toby. I wormed my way through and pulled his sleeve.

'What happened to you?' he shouted in my ear. 'We searched for you and Caroline. Her parents are terrifically steamed up.'

I nodded and smiled at Karen. 'Sorry,' I mouthed. 'Come outside,' I shouted to Toby. 'Just for a minute.'

I dragged him out to the cold night air. Karen went on dancing without him.

'She's cracked completely,' I said. 'I've been walking about with her. She couldn't possibly have played, she's in a terrible state. She's killing herself, Toby! She's anorexic – a long way down the line.' Toby's face registered shock.

'I'm taking her home with me,' I went on. 'She won't let me take her to her own house, but when I get her

131

back I'll ring her parents. Will they have gone straight home, do you think?'

'Yes. They left half an hour ago. God, poor kid. Is she really that messed up? Have you seen Ned? He was looking for you. I'm sorry you've got to go, the party's only just starting. Do you want someone to come with you? I don't think I'd better leave here. I've got to supervise the clearing up.'

'No, I'll be fine. She's exhausted. I'll put her to bed when I get back.'

'Speak to you in the morning,' he said. 'Here,' and he stopped me and kissed me on the lips. 'You were wonderful. A sexy violinist.'

Caroline was crumpled into a corner of my car and in only a few minutes we were back at the farm. I helped her out and into the kitchen where Pilgrim welcomed us ecstatically. Caroline hugged him.

'I'm going to make you a drink and then put you to bed,' I said, getting out a hot-water bottle. 'It will be hot chocolate made with milk and you have got to drink it or I'll ring your parents and get them to come and take you home.'

'Okay, I will,' she said in a tiny voice, meek and submissive. 'I'm sorry I've spoiled your evening.'

'No, you haven't,' I said briskly. 'I'm glad I was there when you needed someone.'

Later on, she slept in my little spare room, hunched exhausted under the duvet, hardly making any kind of mound. While she was in the bathroom I had rung her parents and had a difficult conversation with both. Her mother Geraldine answered, sounding edgy and defensive. According to her, Caroline's behaviour was unforgivable and hugely embarrassing. She asked whether she was ill and if she had a temperature, and why she had wanted to stay with me rather than go home. I explained that her daughter had been very upset and that she had begged me to let her stay the night. Geraldine claimed that she was always seeking attention in this way. I said, 'But you must realise that she is ill. She is quite severely anorexic, isn't she? She told me you knew.'

'I think it's best that you speak to my husband.' She passed the telephone over, but not before she and her husband had exchanged some angry words.

'What is going on?' he demanded. I told him the events of the evening and repeated that I was very worried about Caroline's mental and physical condition.

'Look, this may sound rude after you've clearly tried to help, but what has this to do with you?'

'Nothing at all – I know that. But she needs help and she needed someone tonight. Please get help for her. You must realise how serious this is. You can't ignore or deny it.'

'She has been seeing the doctor, but there is not a problem which we can't deal with. She eats perfectly well at home—'

'She makes herself sick,' I interrupted him brutally. 'She told me. She eats what you give her and then she makes herself vomit. She is also taking packets of laxatives . . . twenty a day.'

There was a silence. When he replied, his voice was no longer aggressive. It was heavy with grief.

'Thank you for having her tonight. I am grateful that she is safe with you. We'll ring in the morning. Thank you. Goodnight.'

When I was eventually lying in my own bed I couldn't sleep. It was strange to have someone else in the cottage. I was conscious of Caroline's brooding unhappiness across the landing. I felt unsettled and disturbed by my dealings with her parents. I thought over the evening, reran the conversations I'd had with Ned, regretted that I hadn't even said goodnight to him.

The telephone rang and I answered immediately, scared that it would wake Caroline up. It was Robert. It was lovely to snuggle down in the dark under my duvet and talk soft words to him. I told him about the evening, and realised as I spoke that I enjoyed my involvement with Caroline and her drama, and rather hated myself for getting some kind of buzz from it. Robert listened with interest. He was sympathetic about Caroline. One of his daughters had been anorexic, had had to leave boarding school because of it and had taken years to recover.

'Who is this Ned?' he asked. 'I don't like the sound of him. You aren't going to fall in love with him, are you? Should I be feeling jealous?' His voice was mild and unconcerned.

'No,' I said. 'There's only you for me. Don't you love me just a little?'

'I'd love to be *with* you . . .' He would never be trapped into giving me the answer I wanted.

A second after I put the telephone down it rang again. This time when I picked it up the line went dead. I was too tired to worry about it and simply turned over and went to sleep.

Chapter Twelve

The next morning Caroline woke at ten o'clock. She came down to where I was sitting in the kitchen with a cup of coffee. Her dusty black clothes of the night before looked more dismal than ever with her face so set and white. Her manner was hostile and closed. Clearly, she regretted the disclosures of the night before. I made her some toast which she cut into minute squares. She refused butter. The atmosphere between us was loaded. I felt compelled to speak.

'Caroline,' I said, and I suppose my voice was full of import because she immediately cut in.

'Don't you start. Please.'

'But Caroline, you've got to get help. You are ill, you know that. You won't get better without help. We agreed all this last night.'

The exhausted sleep of the intervening night had hardened her resolve. She was back to where she was, defensive and denying. 'What do you mean, help? Are you saying I'm mad? That I need a shrink?'

'I'm saying that you won't get better without intervention. That you've got a very serious illness which could kill you. I don't know what its origins are, I'm not an expert, but I do know that it's in your head and that it's like an addiction. Do you see yourself as fat?'

She turned away and shrugged, then answered in a small voice, 'Yeah. Well, I used to be and I still hate this . . .' She screwed a tiny scrap of flesh around her waist. 'Look! It's gross. I'd like to get rid of that.'

'But how much do you weigh? Does the doctor weigh you? How often do you go and see him or her?'

'I've been a few times. He gave me a diet sheet, full of disgusting things like red meat. He did weigh me then – said I mustn't go under seven stone. I think I have a bit. I missed my last appointment because of Mocks.'

'Didn't your mother make you another one? She must have known you'd missed it.'

'No, she was away with Dad on a trip to Hong Kong. She didn't know I hadn't been.'

'Isn't she worried about you? She must be.'

'Yeah. Well, she sometimes goes on about it. She's the one who got me started. Told me I was fat, said I shouldn't wear a bikini on holiday. She's always on a diet herself. Anyway, now she says I've gone too far. She was pleased about it to start with. Thought I looked lots better.' Caroline suddenly looked away and I saw her face crumple. Her hands trembled and she plucked the arms of her sweater down over her knuckles and twisted the end of her sleeves. The world through her eyes was a terrifying place.

'I'm so frightened,' she whispered. 'What can I do? How can I stop? I sort of know I've got to eat but I'm frightened of stopping.'

'Of stopping?' I'd moved round and taken her hand, covered by her chewed cuff.

'Of stopping dieting. Of starting to eat again. I'm frightened of what will happen if I do.' She sniffed and gulped. I gazed at her in utter consternation. What demons occupied her head to make her want to starve herself to death, to see her bony body as fat and unlovable? I found her hand beneath the chewed wool. It was cold and limp.

'Listen, Caroline, all I can tell you is that my best friend at school was anorexic. It dominated our friendship. She

136

was like you, clever and attractive, but she says she always felt unworthy, not good enough and that although she worked very hard and was always top of everything, it somehow wasn't enough. She had to do more, to drive herself harder. She started to eat less and she loved the control it gave her over her body. She began to run and exercise. She was like a fanatic – she *was* a fanatic. It went on for a year before anyone realised what she was doing. At first she was applauded for her discipline and strength of will. We all thought she was fantastic. There we were stuffing ourselves with chocolate after school, worrying about fat and spots, and there she was getting thinner and more wonderful all the time. Then suddenly it had all gone too far. She always wore baggy clothes but we started to notice that she had shrunk away to nothing. Her legs were like sticks. We tried to push her to eat at school but she wouldn't. She just brought in an apple and two pieces of Ryvita.

'One of us eventually spoke to the school about it. In fact, they had already spoken to her parents. She hated us for it; she wanted to be left alone. It took a long time to get her better again. She had to miss the first year at university. You see, they wouldn't take her unless she gained some weight. She went to a clinic once a week in Roehampton, near where we lived. To begin with she cheated and drank pints of water to make herself heavier, put weights in her pockets, all that sort of thing. But they were too clever for her. They'd seen it all before. They explained to her that her devious behaviour was symptomatic of her disease. They were tough on her and absolutely honest. In the end she gave in and accepted that she was an addict and needed treatment. From then on she got slowly better. To begin with they thought that she had damaged her chances of ever having children, but she was okay. She is an estate agent now, married with kids and a great husband. She is happy . . . normal. Not thin, not fat. I remember what it did to her family. Her parents were in despair. There were terrible scenes. They tried to use me as her best friend – thought I could influence her. In the end it got too much for me. There was nothing I could do. She just wasn't there any more. It was like being around a stranger. I remember her father sitting with her as she ate minute pieces of food, tiny tastes of yoghurt, with her weeping all the time. It was a nightmare. Don't let it happen to you.'

Caroline was sniffing, wiping her nose on her sleeve.

'Will you tell Mum and Dad?' she asked. 'Will you tell them about my needing help? About how bad it is,' she crumpled again, 'about how frightened I am? I don't want to die.'

'Yes, I'll tell them.'

I heard a car draw up outside. It was a dull January morning and the grey sky pressed, full of damp, onto the roofs and buildings in the little yard. The windows were beaded with moisture. Toby came to the back door. I glanced at Caroline, wondering if she was ready to see him. 'It's Toby,' I said. 'Would you rather I sent him away?'

'No,' she said, straightening in the chair. 'But don't talk about me, okay?'

'Okay.'

Toby came in, full of cheer. He was accompanied by his little terrier, Buster, who jumped straight on Caroline's knee and licked her hand while Pilgrim frisked about in greeting.

'Are you okay?' Toby asked her.

'Yeah. Sorry about the concert thing. I felt sick.'

I caught Toby's eye and made a 'leave it' face. 'Yes, that's what Harriet said. How do you feel this morning?'

'Okay, thanks. I'm just about to go.' She stood up. 'I don't want a lift, I'll walk. Thanks for having me, Harriet.' And she was gone.

Toby pulled a face. 'Oh God, sorry. Did I come in at the wrong moment?'

'No.' I sighed and got up to make him a cup of coffee. 'It's much too difficult for me to handle. I'm not an expert and she needs counselling. I just hope I've pushed her a bit in the right direction. I'm going to ring her parents now. It seems like bloody cheek on my part, but I shall have to ask them if they really know how bad she is. I gather from what she told me last night that she hardly communicates with them at all. Do you think she'll be okay walking home? Shouldn't we have run her back?'

'It's only a ten-minute walk. If I go after her it looks as if we think she's a risk to herself – a lunatic.' He was right. I looked at his open uncomplicated face. It was all too puzzling for him, beyond his comprehension. 'Why do girls do it?' he asked. 'What is it she's hung up on? I mean, she's like a rake. She can't think she's too fat.'

'Oh, Toby. It's all about body image, about how girls are portrayed by the media, about what they are taught to think is desirable, about what they are led to believe men want. That's how it usually starts, with a desire to lose weight to be more attractive. Caroline's fucking stupid mother put her on a diet, told her that she was overweight, too much puppy fat. Then she was pleased with her when she lost weight. After that it becomes a control thing. What they eat, or what they deny themselves, becomes the one area of their lives they feel good about. Not eating, getting thinner, is the one thing they are confident of. After a while starvation changes the chemical balance in the brain and they stop seeing themselves as thin and become impossible to reason with. By then they are fixed on a course of self-destruction. I just hope that Caroline can be caught in time, otherwise she will kill herself, Toby.'

'How do you know so much about it?' asked Toby as I dialled Caroline's number.

'Because my best friend was an anorexic and I'll never forget it.'

When I telephoned Caroline's parents, it was Geraldine who answered the telephone and this time she was less defensive. As bluntly as possible I told her of my anxieties. I explained that Caroline's temporary break-down of the night before had revealed what I had suspected – that she had a quite advanced eating disor-der. Because I worked in a school with teenage girls, I went on, it was something I had become terribly aware of. The school had a policy to recognise and deal with suspected cases and I felt I must pass on what I knew. Ignoring danger signals was unconscionable.

There was a silence when I pointed out that Caroline had been allowed to miss her doctor's appointment. I could tell that her mother was going through the painful process of having to confront the issue, of accepting that her daughter was ill and in need of specialist treatment. Her own guilt was wrestling to the surface. She knew enough to realise that her relationship with her daughter and other family tensions would have to be revealed, exposed, discussed by strangers. She would find the idea revolting. No wonder it had been easier to deny that the problem existed.

I remembered my friend's calm, controlled mother, who loathed emotional scenes, angrily telling her hus-band that there was nothing wrong with their daughter – that her side of the family were all thin. I felt sorry for Caroline's mother, but not as sorry as I did for her father, the big port-wine faced man whose loudness and confidence had evaporated this morning when his wife passed the telephone to him.

'We love her so much.' His voice cracked. 'What can we do? Has she talked to you? Why is she like this? We've tried everything to—'

'Look, I don't know any of the answers. All I can tell you from my own experience is that when you have acknowledged that there *is* a problem and start to address some of those questions you are both asking, then you are on the way to a cure. But you can't do it alone. I know there is a really good clinic in Bristol because a girl from the school where I teach is having treatment. Your doctor will be able to refer Caroline, I expect. But please don't lose any time. Please ring today. She's desperate. She really is.'

Two days later I had to go to the local surgery to fill in a new patient's form. I was informed that it was practice policy to have a brief interview with the nurse, who happened to be free and could see me right away. She was a brisk woman of fifty, competent, efficient. She nodded approvingly as I said that I was a non-smoker, and as I lied about my alcohol consumption. She filled in family history details, and noted with a frown that my father had died relatively young from a massive coronary. My blood pressure was fine. I took no medication. Yes, I did examine my breasts for lumps, and yes, I did submit to regular, humiliating smear tests. Then she made me stand to be measured and weighed. My heart sank and I felt a wave of familiar panic. This was the moment I used to dread at school. There was no escape. The red needle shot round, wavered, and came to rest. The nurse gazed at it over her half-moon glasses and tut-tutted.

'My word, you're heavy. But then, of course, you're a big girl, aren't you? Still, there is no excuse to be over-weight.' She consulted a graph pinned to the wall. 'At your height, you should be . . .' and she reeled off an optimum weight which I hadn't been since I was sixteen. 'Now,' she said sternly, 'you must either increase your exercise or eat less. How much exercise do you take?'

'Oh, I go to the gym nearly every day,' I lied, 'and of course, as you know, muscle weighs more than fat.'

In my car on the way home I felt a wave of fury. How dare the medical profession treat women like this? How dare that bloody nurse make me feel ashamed, a failure, inadequate? I thought of her flat little chest and straight boyish shape. There was nothing of the woman about her, no hint of flesh, of round thigh or dimpled buttock. Tight-arsed little prig. Twentieth-century marketing had made a woman's natural shape punishable and the medical profession was in league with the fashion industry.

Of course obesity is unhealthy, everyone knows that, but this persecution of larger women is not about health risks. I thought of Caroline starving herself to extinction and my blood boiled against a profession which allows and even encourages women to have boob jobs and nose-jobs; that has spawned a whole branch of surgery devoted to cosmetic enhancement; that allows women to believe their looks can be artificially improved and that the desperate quest for unfading beauty is not only sane but achievable given the right sort of bank balance. This same profession trains a nurse like the one I had just encountered, who with a few short words had reinforced my feelings of hopeless failure and humiliation. It had been these feelings which had driven my friend to starve herself and me to wrestle with a food addiction all my life.

Driving home, I longed to disobey, to rebel, to stop and buy and gorge the contents of the garage shop. It was a small measure of my progress that I reminded myself that the only loser would be me.

When I checked my telephone for messages I found one from Mike asking me if I meant the invitation I had given him to come and stay for a weekend, and if so to call him. The other was from Ned.

'Hi, it's Ned. Just to say hello, and to . . . um . . . sorry, the evening got buggered around. Call in some time if you're passing. Um, better go. Bye.'

What kind of message was that?

I did nothing about it. This was partly because school started for the Easter Term and I was busy during the day. I was now teaching for an afternoon a week at the

Cathedral School, which meant that my overall load was slightly fuller than before. Private instrumental lessons are well paid and I felt gratified that the black hole of my overdraft would soon become less bottomless; before too long, I might even be out of debt. I began to take on more grown-up worries, like paying into a pension fund, and wondering whether my mother's forthcoming marriage would affect me financially.

I was ashamed that this thought had occurred to me, but at the back of my mind was the concern that Douglas might get his hands on her money. I telephoned my sister Isabel, who laughed and said that exactly the same thought had occurred to her. She said she was not concerned for herself, as she and Jake were comfortably off, but she would have liked something to be left to her children. 'What do you make of this Douglas?' she asked.

'He's nice – gentlemanly, but I only met him briefly. Has Ma asked you to meet him?'

'Yes, she has. I'm coming down next Saturday, on the train, to give him the once-over. Shall I get off a stop earlier and come and see you?'

We arranged that I would meet her at the station and we could have a talk about the marriage. As we sat in my car in the station car park, I noted that Isabel looked tired. She said she had had a hell of a week with a very complicated company law case.

'So is it a good thing,' she asked, 'this marrying idea?'

'Well, yes, I think so. It came as a shock to me because I'd never considered Ma as needing a man. I sort of thought her life was fine as it was. She's got us to fuss over and is always busy, or seems to be, you know with the church, her garden, that sort of thing. However she told me that she had been lonely and that the prospect of sharing her life with someone is wonderful. That really bowled me over. I suppose it was incredibly unimaginative of me not to see it before. She had to point it out.'

Isabel laughed. 'I know. One tends to think that emotional needs are the preserve of the under-fifties. Well, if he's nice and she's happy, that's great, isn't it? She deserves it. She's been on her own for so long. It must have been bloody hard. Now, what about the money? I don't actually know the details of Dad's will but I think everything went to Ma for her lifetime. It's that I want to get clear. Make sure that if she pegs it, Douglas doesn't get his hands on it.'

'You can't possibly say that to her. It sounds unbelievably rude and suspicious. We'd upset her dreadfully if we brought it up like that.'

'How can we disguise it? It's what we mean.' Isabel is calm and sensible. She felt we should ask straight out what financial arrangements had been made: it was no good beating about the bush. I balked at this. It seemed like wishing Ma into an early grave. I didn't want to contemplate her death and certainly not talk about it in terms of what money she was going to leave us.

In the end Isabel persuaded me that if I wouldn't allow her to be direct, I should raise the issue on some pretext of needing to know my financial status in case I wanted to buy my first house. She said I was the one who saw most of our mother and that it would seem quite natural coming from me who hadn't a bean to my name. At this moment she had to get out of the car to catch the next train down the line. She kissed me and was gone.

I wasn't at all happy about it. It seemed an impossibly delicate situation. Anything I said would imply that I mistrusted Douglas's motives, and was totally self-seeking. I decided I would put it off.

The other reason I did nothing was because Robert telephoned me that morning with the news that he was going to be in London for two weeks, and I spent every available minute beating up and down the A303 at dawn and again in the evening to spend what time was left with him. I felt drunk with sex and love and I had no time for anything else. We spent every moment either in bed or eating. It was the happiest time of my life.

Helen, I discovered, was away. She was spending three weeks visiting her daughter, Belinda, who was having a year in Australia.

And what of Mike? I am ashamed to say that I had no interest in him and did not even bother to telephone him back. The cottage became dusty and neglected. I had no time to go back there, and for two weeks kept a heap of clothes in the back of my car. Pilgrim settled in happily with my mother, who tactfully asked no questions, and the roots I had started to put down withered and shrank as my new life wheeled off-course. After the two weeks were up, I saw Robert off at Stansted and drove home with a heart like lead. He had kissed me cheerfully goodbye and walked through the barrier without a backward glance: I realised that he was looking forward to getting home.

I collected Pilgrim and unlocked Jerusalem Farm. The kitchen was cold and gloomy. Everything felt damp to the touch. The fridge was empty and there was a loaf grown green and whiskery in the bread bin. A vase of early daffodils, now brown and papery, drooped on the table. The water was stagnant and smelled like a pond. I thought of Mary meeting Robert at Edinburgh Airport, of the venison casserole in the bottom oven of the Aga, of the hot water and the polished taps, the flowers in the hall. I imagined the order and security of his comfortable life. The conversation that would stray over what had happened in his absence. News of their children, that a tree had blown down, that they had been invited to join a party for the Hunt Ball.

I thought of Helen, slim and tanned, staying with old friends outside Melbourne. I imagined her lying on a sunbed by a pool, laughing and sipping a cold drink.

Inside, in the spare bedroom, her carefully chosen clothes would hang, pressed and clean in her wardrobe. I thought of this as I emptied the compost heap of my things out of the back of my clapped-out old car and kicked them about on the floor by the washing machine. I felt engulfed in a wave of self-pity.

This will not do. This will not do at all, I thought.

It took me the rest of the weekend to get things clean and bright and warm again. I polished and dusted and filled the fridge with healthy foods. I put crisp, clean sheets on my bed and filled the window sill with a vase of fresh flowers. I telephoned Mike and invited him for the following weekend. I telephoned Ned, but there was no answer. I telephoned Toby and arranged to meet him for a drink. I telephoned Loops, who said she had flu and wanted to come and stay when she felt better, and I telephoned Caroline, who said she was going to a clinic in Bristol once a week. She sounded very reserved and awkward, and I realised that things were not easy. However, she agreed to come round and see me after school on Thursday. Finally, I telephoned Poppy, who gave me a lecture about neglecting friends and arranged to come and see me when she was down in Wiltshire the following week collecting a chest of drawers she was having stencilled near Tisbury. Poppy's life was now full of such pursuits.

After all this I felt better, more balanced, more whole again. Every time I saw Robert he seemed to wrench the centre out of my life. Poppy told me that I couldn't blame him, that I was doing it to myself. 'All that careering back and forth, staying in a hotel, sex, going out to dinner – that's not real life, is it? It's just an illusion, a diversion. Why can't you see that?'

Of course I saw it. That's what made me miserable. I wanted it to last for ever.

Chapter Thirteen

The next week it rained in great squally clouds and the farm squelched with mud. The sheep looked bedraggled as they stood under the thorn hedge and Pilgrim hated getting his feet wet. Mike's visit was a success. He came on the train because, I was amazed to find, he was a non-driver. He emerged from the station, shambling and untidy, blinking through his thick glasses. His bag was ominously large, but it contained two bottles of whisky and two of wine. He was also struggling with a huge bouquet of flowers – rather nasty ones from a station florist, but a very good effort on his part all the same.

He overlapped with Loops, with whom, needless to say, he fell instantly in love. She had come to me in the middle of the week and spent three days lying in bed, smoking and coughing. By Saturday she was back to radiant health and with a voracious appetite. We cooked messily and drank a lot and watched the rain fall on the grey fields. We discussed Lenten resolutions. Loops was going to give up chocolate and taxis; I didn't want to give up anything. I thought it would be better if I took something up, something improving. We pressed Mike on what he was going to do for Lent. He thought for a bit and said, 'Well, maybe less drink, fewer cigarettes, and . . . some sex.'

Mike loved it when we lit the fire and he could lie on cushions on the floor and watch rugby on the television.

He said it was his idea of heaven when Loops plonked a plate of pasta on his chest and poked him with her foot. 'You are a disgusting slob,' she said. 'Too right,' he replied happily. He was good company.

Loops and I discussed him later as we made a salad while he was outside collecting logs for the fire. 'He's cool,' said Loops, 'but haven't you noticed that less attractive men are much better company, make better mates? They have to put more effort in, see. They can't rely on their looks to pull the chicks. The good-looking guys I meet are either gay or real wankers. Los Wankeros.'

I laughed. She was largely right.

'Your man,' she went on, 'that old man of yours, Roberto. He's both, is he? Attractive and nice with it?'

I smiled smugly and nodded. 'Yes, he is.'

'Yeah, well, believe me, it's rare. Or else love is blind.'

To prove Loops's point, Mike saw that the cottage, Pilgrim and my tentative new life were important to me and he was interested and supportive. He appreciated the food we prepared and without the usual fuss and splashing with which men surround such activities, he took over the washing up neatly and efficiently, even hanging the tea towel to dry on the rail in front of the Rayburn. Loops said that he was so domesticated and nice to live with that it was almost spooky.

Apart from flu, Loops herself was going through a bit of a crisis. She was fed up with modelling and wanted to find something else to do. She had managed to get through a huge amount of money, squandered on clothes, drink and dope, and had little to show for her years on the catwalk and in front of the lens. Now she wanted to go to college and study photography. Mike listened sympathetically and gave her some advice about what to do with the little capital she had left.

Earlier in the week, on her first evening with me, she had met Caroline who had walked over in the dark to see me. I watched as the younger girl took in

Loops's beauty and the lazy attractiveness which worked effectively on either sex. Loops's strong, lithe body emphasised Caroline's frailty. Loops understood at once what the problem was. 'Hey man, you must get your head sorted,' she said. She took Caroline off for a walk in the night, wrapping scarves round her neck before she braved the outside. 'Too much fresh air might be fatal,' she said.

Afterwards, she reported that she had told Caroline how some of her friends had fucked up completely through anorexia; how one of them was still in hospital, where she had been on and off for two years. Caroline had opened up about her own problems, how unpleasant she found the treatment, how hard it was to want to put on weight, how the smallest pressure made her want to revert, to control life through starvation. As Loops told me all this, leaning on the Rayburn, a mug of hot chocolate in her hand, I thought that she had become softer, nicer. Her disenchantment with the posey world of modelling had occurred at the same time as she had become deeper and less superficial as a person. She had dispensed with men for the time being and described it as her Nun Phase.

In front of Caroline, she let rip with some of her back-show stories, and made the other girl laugh. Loops is an excellent mimic and took off the voices and gestures of the foulmouthed girls with whom she worked. 'The aristos are the worst. Christ, they use vocabulary which would make a squaddie blush. All these well-bred types out of boarding schools can't get enough of everything – sex, drugs, drink. They are high on one or other all the time. That's why they're always photographed lolling against a wall or on a sofa. It's because they can't stand up unaided.' She scribbled her telephone number on a scrap of paper and handed it to Caroline. 'Here, give me a ring if you feel like it. Any time.'

★ ★ ★

On Sunday afternoon, after a long walk and a roast chicken lunch, Loops packed Mike into the front of her car and they drove back to London together. Mike said that he'd had a wonderful weekend, and I really felt he meant it. He kissed and hugged me and said he'd keep in touch. He wanted to come again, he said, and offered to decorate the kitchen for me.

I waved them off and turned back into my quiet cottage. Peace settled over the untidy rooms. I was pleased to be alone as I began to empty ash-trays and pick up the scattered Sunday newspapers. As usual I wondered where Robert was. I hadn't heard from him since our love-fest. Just then, the telephone rang. I answered, but no one was there. Damn. I put the receiver down, toying with the idea of ringing the operator and complaining of nuisance calls. Whoever it was who was playing games with me, seemed to be checking whether I was in or not. I even wondered if it could be Robert. Surely not.

That evening as I moved round the house, tidying up and getting ready for the week ahead, I felt Alice with me. Her presence was peaceful, not threatening. Was Sunday evening her one moment of rest? Did she sit by this fire, her workworn hands on her lap, in her best church-going dress, and enjoy the warmth and the darkening room, while her husband coughed out his lungs upstairs? Thinking about Alice, I must have dozed off because I awoke with a start when Pilgrim started to bark. I stood up and listened intently. Going through to the dark kitchen, I put on the light and heard a car turning round in the lane. Lovers, I supposed, looking for a secluded place to park.

I spent that spring half-term in London with Poppy. I was in the middle of an intense Robert crisis. I hadn't heard from him for three weeks. When I telephoned him at home I got his answerphone message. At work, his secretary told me he was unavailable. I rushed to the post each day but there was never anything from him. I felt consumed with anxiety. Why didn't he telephone? Unless he was bound hand and foot and being kept as a hostage somewhere, he could have contacted me somehow. Even a few words would have done. Did the lovely two weeks we'd had together mean nothing? Had they been erased from his memory? Perhaps something awful had happened to him – a coronary, a car accident – but then surely his secretary would have told me?

Helen. Was she behind this? I telephoned his club and asked if he was staying. The receptionist said that he was, and that she would try his room, but then came back to say that he did not appear to be in. I felt a wave of sick despair. He was in London but had not contacted me. I rang Suffolk. Helen's answerphone message said, in her stupid, self-satisfied voice, that she was unavailable but could be contacted on her London number. I dialled it but she did not answer. Another message reported that she was unable to take my call. They were together, I was sure of it.

I caught the Tube and walked to his club. My hands were shaking and I felt sick and distracted. I walked backwards and forwards outside the building and then stood for ages in a doorway opposite where I could watch the people come and go. I am going mad, I thought. If anyone I knew saw me now, they would think I was mad.

I wanted to see him, to catch him cheating on me, but he wasn't cheating. He was not doing anything that he had not already told me about. I went to Covent Garden and at lunchtime stood outside the restaurant they favoured. Twice I thought I saw him, only to find his familiar figure materialise into someone else as it got closer. I eventually went inside and said I wanted to leave a message for him. The girl checked the bookings and said that he had not got a table for that day, or the next. I went back to his club to leave a message there. The porter lent me a biro and gave me a piece of paper. I wrote, *Hello. Have you forgotten me?* And then screwed it up and walked out. I felt too ashamed of my behaviour to tell Poppy. I wasted two days of my life in this futile pursuit.

The Monday of half-term was a lovely day when the sky was a pale mauve and full of soft promises of spring. With great effort of will I forced myself to behave normally. Poppy and I sat in her garden with Tom playing on a blanket in the sun. It was warm enough for him to have bare legs and he waved them in the air like a fat beetle and tried to catch his dimpled toes. Poppy told me she wanted another baby. She said she had grown fond of motherhood and that having babies put off having to make other decisions. I asked her what she meant and she sighed and said, 'Well, you know, motherhood is all, isn't it? Although lots of people have babies *and* jobs, it's perfectly okay not to, to be just a mother. It's like a lovely peaceful backwater where you can drift along in your own world, out of the mainstream. Because we've now got money I can have as much help as I need, so I'm not permanently exhausted like I was with Jess. It's a cocoon, motherhood. I've grown to love it. It keeps the real world at bay.'

'I can see that. Chris loves it, too, doesn't he? I mean, he loves being a father and having you at home with Weetabix stuck in your hair?'

'Heh! I go to a very smart hairdresser twice a week, I'll remind you. But yes, he does love it. He's a provider, a giver and I'm a taker. He needs to give and I need to take, so that's okay. We're well matched. Sex is not great, because I'm never that keen, but it doesn't seem important any more.'

Not important! I thought of my manic journeying backwards and forwards from Somerset to London, paralysed with sexual desire on the outward journey, slack with satisfaction on the return. My relationship with Robert was driven by lust and at the moment he was bonking someone else. My face must have reflected my thoughts.

'What's the matter with you, Hats? You're a bag of nerves. That bloody phone hasn't left your side.' She indicated my mobile. 'Hasn't he called, or something?'

I shrugged and made a face.

'God, why do you put up with it? You are just like a lovelorn teenager. Ring him up and give him a bollocking.'

'I don't know where he is,' I wailed miserably.

'Oh for Christ's sake, get rid of him.'

'It's Helen I want to get rid of. I think he must be with her. God, I could kill her.'

That March my mother got married. She had forestalled the necessity of Isabel and me having to speak to her about her financial affairs, by raising the matter herself.

'Douglas is an old-fashioned man,' she explained, 'and he wants to look after me financially. However, he has children of his own to consider and I am quite well provided for, and so I wish to remain independent. I'm going to sell the cottage and move in with him. His house is larger and has a lovely garden. The proceeds of the sale I intend to invest as a nest egg for my family. Then there is the residue of your father's estate, which I am also leaving to you. It isn't a great deal of money but I intend to pass it over to you now. This is the time of your lives when you need it. Douglas wants to pay for everyday expenses and I have quite enough to keep me in my dotage. I intend to buy myself a place, should I need one, at an Abbeyfield home, so that I won't ever be a burden on you. I wanted to make this clear to you now.'

All this was said on the eve of her wedding. Our brother Iain had come over from America where he is a university lecturer and we had a family party, drinking champagne in our mother's drawing room. She looked so happy and calm as she spoke, I had to sniff and gulp with emotion. Iain, who is large and jolly, not at all academic-looking, put his arm round her and said something about how amazing she had been to us all, and that did it. I started to howl. The others told me to shut up and we drank champagne and became giggly.

Iain's American wife Sally and their four children had not come with him from the States, and so he was staying with our mother. Isabel came home with me. She loved the cottage and sat in my kitchen armchair with her eyes shut. 'I'm drinking in the peace,' she said. 'You've no idea how tranquil this feels compared to my manic household. Our house seems to be permanently in the eye of the storm. Two strong, workaholic characters like Jake and me and three children under twelve do not make for a peaceful environment. I hope you appreciate this, Hats. It's the real plus of being single, you know.'

'I'm beginning to know it,' I smiled as I gave her a glass of wine.

A long uninterrupted bath, which in itself was bliss she said, was followed by delight at the prospect of having a bed to herself. Isabel was asleep at 10.00 p.m. I sat in the kitchen for a while thinking my Robert thoughts. As usual, I tried his number. As usual, his answerphone whirred into action. Oh, Robert, Robert, how can you forsake me?

The following morning a postcard fell out of a pile of bills on the mat. It was from Robert, from Italy. *Darling, darling, girl*, it read. *Wish you were here with me. Thank you for a wonderful time. See you very soon. R.* Italy – Verona. On the front, three fat angels from the Basilica di San

Zeno. It had taken three weeks to get to me. There was a problem with the address. It was covered by a blue pencilled slash and the words *Try Somerset*. He had put Wiltshire. I covered my face with a hand and held the card to my heart. I had been saved.

It wasn't only because of this that Ma's wedding was lovely. The weak spring sun fell on her tiny parish church and Douglas beamed from ear to ear. His three grown-up children who were a bit of an anxiety, Isabel and I had decided, turned out to be perfectly all right. The two sons were straight and tall and clean-cut like their father; they were both in the Navy. His daughter, Tamsin, was fat and cheerful, married to a farmer near Taunton. She had come on her own because she said her children were too horrible to bring to a grown-up occasion, and Phil, her husband, couldn't leave the farm. Mother wore a soft grey suit and no hat. 'I can't be doing with that nonsense,' she said, and together she and Douglas were photographed after the service amongst the nodding daffodils outside the church where he was churchwarden and she organised the flower rota.

Afterwards we went to an expensive country-house hotel, which had grand floral arrangements and squashy sofas and photographs of the owners and their children. I was glad to find that all my anxieties and jealousy had evaporated and that I could be wholeheartedly glad for my mother. Tamsin and I had a brief conversation in the Ladies, standing side by side at the wash hand basins, and she said how much she envied me my profession and independence.

'I married at nineteen,' she confided. 'No training, no qualifications, and now I'm thirty-one with two children at school full-time, and I feel useless. Of course I help on the farm, do the books and so on, and run a little B&B business, but I don't feel I've achieved anything and as if I'm absolutely stuck. I hardly ever leave the place except to shop or take the children somewhere.'

I stared at her in amazement. 'How can you say that? Surely raising children is the most important job in the world!' I thought of Poppy, luxuriating in motherhood.

'Of course it is. I'm not saying it's not, and the kids are the best thing ever, but well, to be frank, financial pressures are so awful just now, and we scrimp and save and just get by, and I don't feel I contribute enough.' Her pretty, plump face collapsed into lines of anxiety. I only had time to make a sympathetic gesture before we were interrupted. I wanted to tell her about adult education and restart programmes designed for women like her, but I didn't get the chance. She sounded tremendously busy, anyway, with two children and all the other things she did, but she had indicated that she felt trapped and undervalued. I told Isabel about this as I drove her to catch her train back to London.

'The trouble is that there's no marketplace value put on being a mother. Who could take over what Tamsin does each day, and if there was such a person, who could afford her? But Tamsin won't feel better about herself until she's got her own little car parked outside and is zooming off to Taunton every day to some ghastly clerical job in a building society. She'll still have to do all the other work as well, and juggle with childcare in the school holidays, but she'll feel it's worthwhile because never again will she have to admit she's "only a housewife".' Isabel sighed. 'I, for one, would have gone completely barmy at home looking after the children. I had about two days off with each and then suffered paroxysms of guilt at leaving them with nannies. But at least I had a choice.'

Poppy was lucky, I thought, that she could enjoy her babies and had the good sense to ignore the pressures to do otherwise. I wondered what I would do if I had children. I romanced for a moment about bearing Robert's child. There was something alluring about the idea of adding a baby to my little household, along with Pilgrim and the sheep.

Chapter Fourteen

The spring began in earnest. For the first time in my life I noticed the days lengthening and the birds beginning to sing in the mornings. In London's neon twilight these things had passed me by. There was a series of nail-bomb attacks of particular ferocity in the city's streets, one going off under a parked car not far from where Chris worked. Poppy rang me, jittery and upset.

'The world has gone mad,' she said. 'London's not safe any more. I worry terribly about the children.'

'Don't exaggerate,' I said. 'London must still be one of the safest capital cities in the world.'

'It's all very well for you to say that. You're highly unlikely to be attacked down where you live, unless there is some group out there targeting the inbred.' I had to laugh, and told her to come and stay for a few days. I wanted to unburden myself to her, make her listen to my stream of misery. I wanted to hear her tell me that Robert wasn't worth it.

'I can't, sweetie. We're going to the opera tomorrow, and Jess is at school now, remember. I don't want to leave her.'

I mooched about unhappily in my garden. I felt sullen with dissatisfaction and at odds with the beauty of the countryside. Pedro's ladies were heavy with lamb and swayed about under the trees eating the sweet young grass. The hedges were swathed with the white blossom of the blackthorn. One afternoon it was hot enough for me to sit on the old bench outside the back door and lift my face to the sun. The next it was snowing. The shepherd came backwards and forwards to the yard, bringing in sheep who had mysteriously aborted on the hill, and others who would not feed their lambs. These ewes were put in a version of the stocks, with their heads stuck through a wooden board to give their lambs a chance at sucking at their bursting bags of milk without being knocked out of the way. It seemed that even in the animal kingdom natural mothering instincts cannot be relied on.

Toby came and went. It was a busy time for him. He had a number of estate properties which required work, as well as the usual land management. He often came to supper, or asked me round to his cottage, or to go for a drink at the pub. When I was with him I managed a façade of cheerfulness; it was when I was alone that the gloom set in. He was booking a group holiday to Sardinia and asked me if I'd like to join. I was unsure because of Robert. What if he wanted me during July? I told Toby I'd let him know.

He took me to the local point-to-point. It was a bitter day and before we left he made me change out of my idea of what one wore to the races, and put on warm trousers and a fur hat. He kindly lent me a window-pane-check shooting jacket. We spent the afternoon in gaggles round people's car boots, drinking vast quantities and neglecting to watch the races, except the Hunt Race which was won by Toby's ex-wife's boyfriend. I was amazed by the acres of tweed and caps and labradors and lurchers and good-looking, long-limbed men and women. They were bold and noisy, shouting with laughter, and the men put their arms round me and it was jolly and loud and the sort of party one would disapprove of as a bystander. When I got an opportunity I asked Toby about Ned; I hadn't seen him

160

since January, not even running past with the push-chair. I hoped he hadn't been ill, or even worse, moved away.

'He's been abroad,' Toby told me. 'He had some work lined up in the States and then went to Poland to set up a dubbing studio. I don't think he's back yet.'

And so we now arrive at the point where I began my story, with murder in my heart. Helen, I had decided, must be behind all this. It was because of her that nearly eight weeks had passed since I last saw Robert. He sent me a second postcard, this time from Germany, and another from the States a week later. On the bottom of each he had written *Will be in touch on return.* Yet he still has not telephoned. I have left messages on his answermachine in Scotland and with his secretary in London and at his club. He has effectively vanished. I ring Helen's number and am always rewarded with her answermachine.

Where have they gone? I am convinced they are together. Eventually, I telephone his home number. I am going to ask Mary where he is. I don't care any more about the risks or what she will think. I'll pretend I am some sort of colleague. A female Scottish voice answers and tells me that Mr and Mrs Mackintosh are on holiday in Spain for two weeks. Ah! I feel weak with relief. At least he isn't with Helen. I can forgive Mary her time with him.

The knot that twists in my stomach loosens and I am able to get on with my life without feeling sick and panicky. I had convinced myself that he was trying to get rid of me, that by allowing communication to slip he was gently easing me out of his life. One evening last week when I was feeling particularly despairing I had collected all my mementos of our time together – the theatre and concert tickets, the corks from the bottles we had shared, the napkins on which he had scrawled

161

me messages of lust – and thrown the lot into the fire. Now I regret their passing. It is all going to be all right. I do not push myself to answer the question of why he treats me in this way, or how easy it would have been for him to let me know where he is. I want to look on the bright side, to accept the best possible interpretation of his actions. I want him back. My life is nothing without him.

The telephone exerts a terrible influence. I cannot bear being in the same room as the silent instrument. My mobile is constantly with me. Every time it rings my heart leaps and I am always disappointed. I cannot bear to hold a conversation with anyone who is not him. I am short with Loops, with my mother, with Poppy. At other times I need to talk, to relieve the anxiety. I am caught in a private hell. He's not worth it, I tell myself. I am worth more than this. He loves Helen. Helen, Helen.

I have to go to work and I make myself be marginally sociable. I go out with Toby and have dinner with Mike. It is the general routine of ordinariness that will save me from this pitching sea of emotions.

Eventually, when I have almost given up, he telephones.

He is as warm and friendly as ever. It has been impossible, he says, to contact me. He had on various occasions tried to telephone but I was always out. I narrow my eyes at this. I check my telephone messages so assiduously and dial 1471 with such true obsession that I don't believe him. But I forgive him. He says he needs to see me and we arrange a dinner date in London for the end of the week.

My heart sings and I go into the usual routine of starving myself and preparing to look my best. I take Pilgrim to my mother's and cut my last lesson on Friday and drive to London. The traffic is heavy coming the other way, but I am migrating against the tide and sail along. I sing and smile at the other drivers. The men smile back and flash their headlights. I feel beautiful and blessed. I even find a parking space near the restaurant and time it exactly right.

Robert is there waiting for me. He kisses me warmly and I settle into the chair opposite him. He looks tanned and well. He is wearing a beautiful shirt of very expensive, heavy cotton in a delicate herring-bone weave, and a matching tie and handkerchief. He takes my hand across the table. I wonder, irrationally, if he is going to ask to marry me. We talk in hurried bursts, both asking how the other has been. I smile a lot. My looks are sweet and coquettish. He loves me: I know it. He has an air of excited expectancy about him, as though he has something important and wonderful to say. Five countries have been visited in as many weeks. It has been hectic, he says, and then this holiday with Mary. They have had ten days in Spain together and it is this he needs to tell me about.

'Why? What happened?' I am suddenly unsure of what is to come. 'Has Mary found out about us? Is it all in the open?'

'No, nothing like that. Well, not exactly like that.' He looks rather smug and satisfied.

'What do you mean?' I ask, my throat tightening in panic. I can feel a flush creeping up my neck. He leans across the fills my glass and then, maddeningly, consults the menu and asks me what I want. I sit with my hands in my lap as we go through this rigmarole. I am quiet and obedient, meekly waiting. I can see he is playing for time, that what is to come is tricky. He is searching for the right words.

'Is it Helen?' I ask. 'Is this about her?'

'Indirectly,' he says smoothly. 'I saw her this morning.' My stomach lurches. It's Helen. He is going to marry Helen.

'What is this about? For God's sake . . .'

163

'Let me tell you.' He tastes his wine. 'Ah! Delicious. An excellent year for white Burgundy.' I sigh and raise my eyes impatiently. He takes a mouthful of wine and works it round his mouth. It pleases him and he smiles. He begins what he has to say to me. He has no difficulty in holding my hand across the table. He massages it with his thumb. He tilts my chin up with his other hand. Smiles into my face.

'As you know, Mary and I have just been on holiday. In fact, it was Mary's idea that we did, and she booked the parador. It was the most beautiful place, and as we usually do on holiday, we shared a room – a double bed, in fact. I later found out that Mary had requested this, and it dawned on me that she intended to seduce me. I told you from the beginning that she is an attractive woman and that I still fancy her? She's well-preserved. Good figure. Excellent legs. Well, I was delighted. Having sex lent a new intimacy, a closeness we haven't enjoyed for years. She asked me about my relationships with other women and I confessed that they had been pretty continuous since she had stopped looking after me herself. She said she had suspected that this was the case. I glossed over my amours as well as I could, told her nothing specific. It's more painful to be told too many details, I think – don't you? The only thing marginally in my favour in her eyes is that I have taken some care in my choice of mistresses – no one she knows or is ever likely to meet. At least I've spared her that indignity.'

Hmm, I think, hating him, very thoughtful.

'Eventually we struck a bargain. Both of us want to continue with our marriage, but we feel it deserves a fresh start. I have promised Mary that I will give up my girlfriends if she will share my bed. And so, my dear, this is what I've come to tell you. I shall miss you enormously and I have to say I have my doubts as to how long this truce will last, but I must give it a chance

164

to work.' He smiles gently. My face feels stiff from smiling. He is sacrificing me for Mary.

'And Helen? Have you given her the boot as well?'

'Yes. She is, I am sorry to say, very angry. Devastated. She feels I have made a great mistake. She admits she always nursed a hope that I would divorce Mary and marry her, although I have always been scrupulous in denying that this was ever a possibility. She is a woman who is used to getting her own way. Quite spoilt, in fact. Yes, she's angry.'

I push aside the plate that the waiter is trying to set down in front of me. I need to get out. I scrape back my chair and stand up. The surprised waiter and I are standing side by side. He is still holding my plate. Robert looks up, mildly troubled.

'Are you going? Oh please, stay and eat. I was looking forward to your company.'

I sit down again. Relieved, the waiter slides my plate in front of me. Robert takes my hand.

'I shall have very fond memories,' he says, 'of my beautiful violinist.'

My mind is blank. I grope around for a genuine feeling but there is none. My head seems empty. I pick up my glass. There are no tears. I can't touch any anger. I feel as long-drawn-out and as feeble as a length of string. I find my voice and manage to say, shakily: 'Here's to you and Mary. At least it's not Helen who has won.' I take pleasure in Helen's anger. I am glad that she is hurt.

'Yes – Mary. She's really rather remarkable.' He smiles, pleased. 'She's a strong woman.'

Suddenly I see it, the bare bones of his relationship with Mary. The naughty boy is forgiven and taken back. The Prodigal returns. Robert goes home.

Unlike Helen, I behave well. It seems he wants to sleep with me one last time. I give in. It's better than ever. He is cheerful and buoyant. I feel empty. It is only sexual desire that I can rely on. My body is treacherous in its response. Truthfully, as I lie in his arms I am not sure that I really care that this will be the last time. I feel scraped clean. The next morning he gets up ready to go to the airport. He kisses me goodbye.

'We'll keep in touch,' he says. 'Friends?'

'Yes,' I say. 'Friends.'

He is gone.

I don't want to speak to anyone. I drive home feeling nothing. I collect Pilgrim and go back to Jerusalem Farm where I systematically remove any trace of Robert. I ring Toby and tell him I'd like to go to Sardinia. My telephone rings four times. Each time there is no one there.

Chapter Fifteen

Two months have gone by since I started my story, but the events of the morning following that last meeting with Robert are clearly defined in my memory. Ned and I often talk over what happened. He listens patiently, understanding that he is the only one I want to share it with. Of course, at the time, I did not realise that anything significant was going to happen, but the fact that my life was shortly to be changed has illuminated everything that went before so that the most everyday of actions has become imbued with significance.

It started as a perfectly normal Sunday morning. I had woken early after a restless night in which my mind went round and round everything that had passed between Robert and me. It was hard to believe that this time yesterday I was waking in bed with him and now he had gone out of my life for ever. I felt surprisingly calm and resigned. In a way I knew that I had had enough, that I was sick of it all.

I went downstairs to make a cup of tea and let Pilgrim out, as I always did. It was a disappointing sort of morning and the bricks outside the back door glistened with a greasy dampness. As I waited for the kettle to boil, I leaned my elbows on the kitchen counter and read the back page of yesterday's newspaper. The kitchen door stood open and I could hear the clamour of the sheep in the yard behind the cottage and the high-pitched voices of the lambs. Rooks cawed. Some-where in the village a distant dog barked.

The kettle boiled and I poured the water into my little blue teapot, then I collected milk and cup and saucer and put them on the small tray which I use every morning. Taking down the biscuit tin for Pilgrim's morning treat, I went to the back door and called him. The fact that he wasn't already back inside was slightly unusual, particularly on a wet morning, but not enough to alarm me. He often took his time. I called him again and because my bare feet were cold on the floor, I left the door open and went back upstairs to bed. I love my bed, I can remember thinking as I climbed in and plumped up my pillows so that I could sit comfortably. I wanted to think about yesterday. I needed to resolve how I felt, what emotions I could justify. I thought of Robert waking up in Mary's bed. Scratching and farting and taking up a lot of space, Mary, bony and cold, beside him. It almost made me laugh. I poured out my tea. The tray lay on the other side of the bed nearest the door.

The noise I heard then was not in itself frightening. Many times I've heard exactly that same sound, but in this context it moved me to instant alarm. It was the noise of human feet running fast up my wooden stairs. Almost as soon as I heard it and identified it, a figure appeared in my door, which stood open. For a moment I thought the woman who hesitated for only a second needed help, that there had been an accident. I took in briefly that she was small, slight, pale-faced with cop-pery, synthetic-looking bobbed hair. Her expression was extraordinary – her features distorted by terrible malice. Then almost simultaneously I saw she had a largish knife – a kitchen knife – in her right hand and that she was holding it, blade pointing straight down, at breast height. Her other hand was also raised, but palm for-ward and fingers splayed. The expression on her face was one of pure hatred. I instantly understood her intention to harm me and I screamed, I think, and stumbled out of bed on the other side, as she lunged forward, knocking over the tray of tea. She was shouting something incoherent.

Instinctively I knew I must not be trapped in a corner and I rushed to get past her and out of the door. She caught hold of my arm as I went and the knife slashed down across my shoulder. I gave her an almighty shove and she fell back a little and I broke free and made for the stairs. She was smaller than me, lighter, older. I had the advantage. She caught hold of my nightdress and yanked me back but I swung round and hit her as hard as I could in the face. She let go and I fell down the stairs. At the bottom she was just behind me, clutching at my arm. I turned and kicked her but she jumped back and slashed down with the knife. A spurt of red bloomed on my nightdress. My breath was coming in great gasps and all the time I was screaming as well.

She rushed at me again but I had snatched up a lamp and threw it at her. It was anchored by its flex and fell short. I grabbed an armchair and pushed it between us while looking round wildly for something to defend myself with. My music stand was in the corner. I reached it just as she climbed round the chair to get me. I fended her off by swinging the stand in front of me. I was angry and aggressive myself now. I slashed at her with the stand and caught her in the face. She screamed and held a hand to her eyes. I slashed again. She was in retreat, still holding the knife but somehow collapsed and defeated. She gave ground every time I advanced. I was pushing her back to where the kitchen door stood open. A few more paces and I'd have her out.

At the step, she tripped backwards, but seemed to rally her strength and made a wild grab for my hair, still holding the knife as if she was going to stab me in the face. She dragged me outside with her. I swung the music stand round and, although it felt as if she was going to rip my hair out by the roots, I jammed it into her upper chest. She slipped, lost her balance and stepped back, straight onto the slope down to the cellar. The change of level took her by surprise and she teetered backwards. Another shove from me and she careered back, straight through the open wooden door. I followed her like a flash and slammed the door shut and shot the bolt.

Still terrified, I scrambled on all fours up the ramp; my nightdress was stuck to my thigh with blood and I was shaking. I was too frightened to go back inside and started running away down the lane, towards the village. My legs worked but only just. Every now and then my knees gave out and I nearly fell. I heard feet behind me and I started to scream as I ran. They came closer, catching me up. Too terrified to look round, I kept on. I could see someone in the distance. At the same time as I realised it was Ned coming towards me, I also understood that I was being followed by Pilgrim. Not given to fainting, I collapsed onto the road on my knees. My hair hung forward over my face. Pilgrim whined and tried to lick me. When Ned finally reached me I never saw the expression on his face because I was being sick in the ditch.

The next hour or so passed in a blur. Ned reached me and thought I had been involved in some sort of accident. He took off his sweatshirt and made me put it on. I realised later that my nightdress was nearly ripped in half and my left breast was completely exposed. He tried to gently lead me back to Jerusalem Farm but I screamed, 'No, no! She's still there!' and it slowly dawned on him that I'd been attacked. I was still crying and barefooted and he didn't want to leave me to get help and so he put his arm through mine and supported me down the hill towards his cottage, making encouraging noises and stroking my hair. 'Look, you're okay. You're not badly hurt. You're okay. It's all right now.' Desperately he looked to see if there was a car coming in either direction. After five minutes or so, the red post van appeared and pulled up. The postman looked white-faced.

'Bloody hell!' he said. 'What's going on? There was a madwoman shut in the cellar back at the farm. I've just let her out – screaming blue murder, she was.'

'You haven't let her out?' I choked. I clutched Ned's arm. 'Oh my God, he's let her out. Oh my God!'

'Quiet, quiet. You're safe now,' said Ned. 'She's been attacked,' he told the postman. 'That woman went for her with a knife.'

'Well, she's gone now – took off in a white car. I got the number. How was I to know, anyway? I thought it was you shut down there. Thought maybe the door had slammed shut. Bloody hell. You'd better get in and I'll take you to Mill Cottage.'

Ned bundled me in amongst the letters and parcels and squashed in beside me. He lifted my nightdress to look at the cut on my thigh. The blood was trickling down my leg and I felt sick and faint. The postman kept glancing at the letters, worried that I was going to bleed over them.

It took only a few minutes to drop us off at Ned's cottage and in a moment I was in his warm kitchen and he was rummaging around looking for brandy and getting bowls of water and Dettol and cotton wool. He went through to the hall and rang the police, to report what had happened. 'No, I don't think it's a domestic, as you call it,' I heard him say. 'She was just attacked by a madwoman she doesn't even know.'

'I do know her,' I shouted through the door to where he stood in the hall. 'I do! I know who she is.'

'Okay! Okay! You can tell them when they come,' he shouted back at me. He was gone for ages. I heard him spelling out his name and address. He couldn't remember my surname, didn't know his postcode. When he came back into the kitchen he said, 'God! What a performance. Anyway, they are on their way. Look, you're going to have to let me bathe your leg.'

I felt completely unmoved that I was sitting semi-naked in the home of a man I barely knew while he bathed my thigh and wiped the stream of water from my leg. He was so gentle and kind. I looked at his shiny, floppy hair as he bent over me. It was threaded with silver and I wanted to touch it. He looked up and smiled, relieved that I was calmer.

'Hang on,' he said, and he dashed off and came back with a dressing gown which he helped me put on. I noticed it had his name sewed on the inside on a school name tape. He told me that the cut wasn't deep and had stopped bleeding, 'Although it may need a stitch or one of those butterfly things. I'm going to call the surgery.'

But first he poured us each two inches of brandy into a coffee mug. Then he put the kettle on.

'Hot sweet tea,' he said comfortably. 'That's the thing for shock. Brandy first, while the kettle boils.'

When he went to telephone the doctor, Pilgrim came and laid his head on my knee. He was shuddering with emotion.

'Pilgrim's having a breakdown,' I managed to say through chattering teeth.

'Oh God,' said Ned, 'you're still freezing – it's shock, I expect. Listen, the surgery isn't open on Sundays. I should have thought of that. I've spoken to the duty doctor who says you should go to Accident and Emergency in Salisbury: they'll see you there. But we have to wait for the police. Hold on.' He dashed off again and came back with a blanket which he wrapped me in.

While we were waiting for the police to arrive I told him briefly that I'd been attacked by the mistress of someone I knew. In a jealous rage, I supposed.

'Someone you know?' he echoed. 'Do you mean a lover?'

'Well, yes. But not really a lover as you'd know it. We hardly saw one another, and in fact he finished it yesterday. He's gone back to his wife.' I took a big swig of brandy and felt it scorch down my throat. I noticed my mug had *Ned* written on the side in thick white writing. He leant forward and kissed me.

'You're so brave,' he said. 'You're great! You'll be okay, Harriet.'

'Thank God you weren't pushing Dido,' I said, suddenly struck by a thought. 'Can you imagine . . .?'

'I don't have her on Sundays. Nicky doesn't work today.' He picked up my hand and started to rub it between his, and then tucked the blanket more securely round me. 'Thank heavens you're okay. That woman – was she really trying to kill you? Who the hell is she, anyway?'

'Her name is Helen. I don't know if she was trying to kill me, but it seemed like it. She had a damn good try.'

The police took ages. They laboured through my statement and then said that they wanted me to accompany them back to Jerusalem Farm. Ned said he would come with me. I was relieved to find that when I got out of the police car I didn't feel frightened to walk with the two officers and Ned along the path which I had so recently fled. The music stand was lying on its side in the grass. The cellar door swung in the wind. I pointed it out.

'There. That's where she fell . . . she sort of tottered backwards. I slammed the door shut after her – that's what saved me. It's peculiar. It's never been open before.'

We went inside the cottage and surveyed the scene. There was the armchair askew in the sitting room, the lamp rolled on the floor on its side . . . otherwise one would never have believed that a drama had so recently taken place. We went upstairs and I showed the two officers exactly what happened. They seemed to want me to remember what my attacker had screamed at me, but I couldn't.

'It was just a sort of incoherent stream of invective – "bitch", things like that.'

'So would you describe yourself as her rival?' asked the older, grey-haired man. He was fatherly, kind. He treated the bizarre events as neither shocking nor surprising. I imagined him shutting his notebook and saying, 'All in a day's work.' I supposed that he had often to deal with domestic dramas. Road accidents. Sudden deaths. An hysterical young woman with scratches on her leg inflicted by a rival lover was no big deal.

'Well, I was once, slightly. Not any more. It was over. Finished.'

'Helen Caplan,' mused the policeman. 'Do you have an address?'

'I have a telephone number. The postman has her car registration number.'

'Yes. We've got his statement and have put a tracer on that.'

At that point I asked them if I could go and get dressed. I spent five minutes washing my face and brushing my hair, and I managed to put on a skirt and a sweater. I could hear Ned talking to the police and when I went back down he had made tea and the three men were in the kitchen. I felt rather shaky. I didn't know whether I should be smiling bravely or what.

'Sorry,' Ned said, indicating the mugs, 'didn't want to bother you. Would you like a cup?' It was odd seeing him moving round my kitchen, opening cupboard doors while the officers went through everything again.

The patrol-car radio cackled and the older man went outside. We drank tea and Ned and the younger policeman started to talk about football. I felt remote and suddenly tired. I wished they'd all go. When the older man came back his face was changed. It looked grimmer, closed.

'Mrs Helen Caplan has been out of the country since last Friday – she's on holiday in Tunisia. The car belongs to a Mrs Rachel Pearson. She has just been picked up at a Little Chef outside Salisbury. The manager called us to a woman who appeared to have had some sort of mental breakdown. We've got her in custody. Later we'd like you to come with us and identify her. But now we'd better go through this story again.'

Ned stared at me with his mouth open.

'But I don't know a Rachel Pearson,' I told them, baffled. 'I've never heard her name before today, and I've certainly never seen her before today. I promise you, I don't know her. Was it just a random lunatic attack? Why me? And all those telephone calls I've been getting which went dead – I'm sure it was her. She's been stalking me. It's so weird.'

Later, I repeated all this to Ned who was kind enough to drive me into Salisbury Hospital. The police had offered to take me, but Ned had stepped in.

'You don't want to go through this on your own,' he said, and then after a hesitation: 'Look, do you want to contact your family? Your mother lives around here, doesn't she?'

'Yes, she does, but I don't want to involve her. She doesn't know anything about this man, you see, and she's just got remarried. My best friend lives miles away in London, and I'm not keen to involve her either. It would be really kind if you'd stay with me for a bit. Thanks, Ned. Honestly, I appreciate it.'

So here we were in his van, bowling along through thatched and peaceful villages.

'Why were you so sure before that it was this Helen woman?' he asked. 'Has she threatened you or something?'

I thought for a moment. I'd already been through this

175

with the police. 'No, she hasn't.'

'What – not on the telephone, or by letter? No confrontation over this man? Who is he, anyway?'

'No. Actually I've never had a conversation with her; I've never met her, or spoken to her. The man isn't important. As I've told you, it's over. He finished it yesterday. It had come to an end.'

'So – let me try and get this straight. You are attacked by some unknown unhinged woman and you say with great confidence that you know her identity. Yet the woman you accuse has never met you or had any contact with you?'

'Yes, that's it. But I *thought* she would want to kill me – if she found out about Robert and me, or thought he had ditched her because of me. He's just finished with her too, apparently.'

'Look, sorry if I'm being immensely dense, but on what grounds did you think she would react like this? It's a bit extreme to want to kill one's rivals.'

'Oh, a number of things,' I said vaguely. I hated having to articulate the truth. Held up to the cold light of day I realised that the assumptions I had made about Helen were without any foundation . . . the stuff of fantasy.

Ned shook his head in disbelief. 'None of it makes sense,' he said. He looked at me shrewdly. 'Are you telling me the whole truth? Is there something more going on here? I realise that I don't have any claim to know, but I'd like to think you'd confide in me.'

'Ned, I promise I have no idea who this woman is, or why she attacked me. There's nothing more to tell. If she's not Helen, then I don't know who she is.'

'Okay,' he said, and patted my knee.

We were silent for a bit and then I said: 'It's horrible. I feel sort of dirtied by this. It seems so – well, sordid, to be involved in a violent attack, as if it's my fault. I kept wanting to say that I was sorry to the police. I felt they were disapproving – judging me, somehow.'

'Why should you feel that? You're a completely innocent victim.'

Am I? I thought. I changed the subject. 'Tell me about you, Ned. We've never really had a chance to talk. Tell me about Nicky and Dido. Are you separated? Divorced?'

Ned took his eyes off the road to look sideways at me. 'Divorced? For goodness' sake, Nicky's my sister!'

'Your sister? I didn't know that. From the way you talked, looking after Dido like you do, I thought you must be married.'

'A lot of your assumptions seem to be wrong,' he said, not unkindly. 'You see, Nicky's husband Tom was killed in a car crash about three months before Dido was born. It was ghastly. Nicky and I have always been very close and I just supported her as much as I could. When I moved down here she was just starting to get her life back together again and had this part-time job lined up. I offered to help with childcare. It wasn't hard for me. I was mucking about working at home and at that stage Dido wasn't particularly demanding. In fact, I've loved helping with her. She's about to start at some sort of battery farm for children in September, and so it will all come to an end soon. I'll be redundant.'

'Ah. I see. God, I got that all wrong, didn't I?'

'You did indeed.' Ned smiled at me. 'Me – married? Dream on!'

'Why, don't you want to be?'

'If I found the right person. Just never have. Not anyone that wanted me, either. I'm obvious father material though, aren't I? What about you? Was this bloke important to you?'

I considered. 'Yes, he was. I'm just getting used to the idea that he's gone.' I sighed. 'The truth is that I was never that important to him. I sort of lived a fantasy for five years.'

177

Ned patted my knee. 'He must be mad.' It was a meaningless, comforting thing to say but I was grateful.

The Accident and Emergency department was still quiet. The Saturday-night emergencies had been dealt with and the Sunday gardening and sporting accidents had yet to get under way. An old woman like a shrunk pixie with straggling grey hair was weeping in a wheelchair with her leg in bandages. A black nurse knelt at her side saying, 'You're all right now, dear. We'll look after you.' A young man with a smashed face was sitting on a plastic chair accompanied by a gum-chewing girlfriend with platinum hair. Ned took me to the admissions desk where we filled in forms and I was told to join the others in the waiting room. Ned disappeared to get coffee and when he returned I had already been called into a cubicle to be seen by an extremely young doctor in a check open-neck shirt and unbuttoned white coat. He looked tired and distracted. I suspected he'd been on call all night.

'So how did this happen?' he asked as he removed Ned's makeshift bandage and examined my cut.

'I was attacked,' I said, 'with a knife.' He looked up, surprised. I could see him wondering about me. Probably he thought I was the victim of a brutal husband or boyfriend. I didn't offer any more information and he busied himself with swabs and some stinging liquid and asked me about tetanus injections.

'I'm not going to stitch it, just put on these butterfly plasters. It's not very deep and should heal quickly. Now, do you have any other injuries?'

I showed him the scratches and bruises on my arm and neck.

'We don't need to do anything for these,' he said. 'They are superficial. How do you feel? You'll suffer from shock, you know, and I'm going to prescribe you some sleeping pills. Go easy on yourself for a few days. Where do you work? Do you want a sick note?'

I mumbled something vaguely and said I didn't. The last thing I wanted was to be moping around with nothing to do. Ned put his head round the curtain, holding the plastic coffee cups.

'Can I come in?' he asked.

The doctor looked at me for a reaction, obviously wondering if it was Ned who had attacked me.

'We're finished,' I said, and smiled at him. I got off the bed and stood up. 'Thank you, Doctor.' I was grateful that he hadn't made me feel contaminated. A nurse stuck her head round the curtains.

'Miss Lennox? There's been a call from the police. They want you to go straight to the police station when you're finished here. They've got the woman who attacked you.'

The police station was large and intimidating. Ned waited with me while the desk sergeant sorted out an interview room. A WPC came to collect me and took me to a viewing room. Through the glass window in the far wall I saw a weeping woman. She was small and thin with flat reddish hair. Her face was streaked with mascara. She was wringing her hands and rocking from side to side.

'Yes,' I said. 'That's her.' I felt unsettling to see the person who had frightened me so much and who had violated my home with such pure hatred and aggression now reduced to a small desolate figure rocking on a plastic chair. Why had she wanted to see me dead? I thought of a different outcome, of my body slumped on the floor, of the cottage cordoned off, a flurry of police cars with flashing blue lights. How close had I come to being a murder statistic?

I was taken back to Ned and we waited for an hour or so. A policewoman made us another cup of tea. Finally the superintendent came to collect us and took us into his office.

'So far so good,' he said. 'We have a few more pieces for the jigsaw puzzle. The woman you have identified as your attacker is Mrs Rachel Pearson, aged forty-nine, divorced, of 43, Chalfont Street, Osterly. She is employed as a secretary in a firm of music publishers, Mackintosh and Grove.'

'Ahhh!' I gasped and closed my eyes. Now I understood.

'It seems your, um, erstwhile friend Mr Mackintosh has also been intimate with Mrs Pearson. Apparently she turned to him for comfort during an unpleasant divorce and he enjoyed a relationship of sorts with her over a period of nine years. Some time ago he brought this to a close. Mrs Pearson knew of your existence and saw you as a rival for Mr Mackintosh's affections. She felt that you had a role to play in her losing him. She said she had no intention of seriously harming you: she only wanted to frighten you. She has suffered from depression and is undergoing a course of treatment from her doctor. We have contacted him and he claims that this behaviour is utterly out of character. However, he has agreed that we should attempt to have her sectioned under the Mental Health Act in a secure hospital for a period of three weeks while we can assess her condition. Personally, Miss Lennox, I am unwilling to press charges. Whilst this does have the characteristics of a much more serious incident, there was no breaking and entering; Mrs Pearson gained access through an open door and the weapon involved, although it looks dangerous and was capable of causing the wound on your leg, is, in fact, a plastic toy.' And he laid the knife on the table. 'We found it in her car.'

Ned and I gazed at the grey plastic blade. It looked absurdly unreal. And yet I had been so frightened. I felt foolishly disappointed, as if I had been duped.

The superintendent went on, 'You also have to consider whether you are happy to face the attendant publicity this case would involve – media interest and the like. I see you work at the girls' school in Salisbury.' He paused. 'How would your headmistress feel about this being raked over in the press? I think you should consider these aspects and I will contact you on Monday. If, however, you wish to go ahead and press charges for assault you will have our full support.' He stood up. Ned and I followed suit. I wanted to get out, to digest the information I had just been given. As we passed through the entrance hall a young woman, visibly upset and supported by a young man in a leather jacket, was saying to the duty sergeant, 'You've got my mum. You telephoned me. I can't believe it. She's in some sort of trouble . . .'

We were silent on the way home. I felt incredibly gloomy. How had my most personal life, a love affair I thought of as nobody's business but my own, ended up as evidence, recorded in factual and unsympathetic language in a police statement? Finally, Ned said, 'Are you going to be all right on your own? Do you want to stay with me? It's full of mess, but I've got a spare room.'

'Ned, I'll be fine. *Fine*. I'm okay now I know that I wasn't nearly murdered. Just drop me off. I can't thank you enough.'

He insisted on coming in with me. He pushed the armchair back into place and picked up the lamp. He made up the stove and filled the hod with coke. Much as I appreciated his kindness I wanted to be alone. I was glad when he finally left, still anxious and solicitous.

Left alone I sat in the kitchen. It was three o'clock. Pilgrim rested his head on my knee. It was very quiet. I could hear the sheep in the yard and rooks cawing in the wood just as I had done in the morning before all this had happened. The cottage seemed to have absorbed the violence of the day. Wearily I got up and cleared away the tea mugs and straightened things up. I locked the kitchen door, filled a hot water bottle and went upstairs to where my bed lay in its violated state with the upset tea tray. The cup Robert had given me had fallen to the floor and the handle had broken off. I picked up the pieces. The pretty French porcelain was old and cracked. Sadly I put it into the wastepaper basket. I didn't want it any more. I forced myself to change the sheets, then I closed the curtains, took the phone off the hook and swallowed one of the sleeping pills which Ned had insisted I collected from a chemist in Salisbury. Pilgrim got on the bed and burrowed under the duvet.

Much later, I was woken by a loud banging and lay for a moment rigid with fright. Gradually I remembered where I was. The light was subdued in the crack between the drawn curtains. I looked at my watch: it was after eight o'clock. The banging went on and I heard a man calling my name. I rolled out of bed and started down the stairs, still doing up my jeans.

Ned stood looking upset in the porch by the front door. 'God!' he exclaimed when I opened the door. 'I've been so worried. I've been knocking for ages. Your telephone has been permanently engaged. Are you all right?'

'Yes, I'm fine. I was just asleep, that's all. I can't believe I've slept for so long.' I ran my hands through my tangled hair. 'Come in.'

He stepped inside and put his arms round me. Weakly, I buried my face in his jumper. 'I just had to find out if you were all right. I've been trying to telephone. I was going to ask you to supper.'

I began to cry. My head was swimming from the pill, I suppose, and I felt feeble and pathetic.

'I don't know why I'm crying. I'm sorry,' I sniffed.

'Don't say sorry. It's fine to cry – good to let it out. You've had two pretty traumatic days.'

I couldn't bear his kindness. I turned away and stood with my head in my hands, shaking with sobs. He put his arms round me, tenderly.

'It's okay. It's okay,' he said, stroking my hair.

'No, it's not. It's all so horrible, so *sordid*! That Rachel woman and her misery, her depression. Her poor daughter. Their lives torn apart. All this wreckage, and I'm part of it. How did I let it happen? And there's more. There's Mary, his wife and his children. And there's Helen . . . God, I just want out of it all; I want to be free of it. But now I'm in it up to my neck. The police and all that.'

'That's not true. You don't have to press charges – they told you that. You can just let it go. It can all be over if you want.'

'Yes.' I sniffed and wiped my eyes. 'Sorry. A moment of self-pity, and self-judgement.' I managed a smile. 'God, I'm starving. Do you fancy sharing a tin of beans with me?'

'Well, I don't wish to force my company on you. I just thought you might not want to be alone.'

'You're so kind,' I said. 'I keep having to thank you.'

We had a beans-on-toast supper and drank quite a lot of red wine which Ned had been given by a client; it was still in a case in the back of his van. Over the course of the evening I told him a bit more about Robert and Helen and the mess I had got my life into, and how I was trying to get back on course. I realised that I minded what he thought of me. He told me about his work and how he felt isolated and often lonely working from home. When he said he must go it was already Monday morning. I was tempted to suggest he stayed, but I said nothing. From now on I was not going to allow my life to be controlled by impulses. We kissed briefly and then again.

'I'll ring you tomorrow,' he said.

'Yes, please,' I answered.

The next day I had to face work. Although it was so late, I tidied up the cottage and wondered what I was going to wear. I thought about Alice as I moved from room to room. Had the disturbances of the morning upset the peace of the cottage permanently? Had the violent emotions for ever charged the atmosphere of the old rooms? I didn't think so. The cottage seemed to embrace me in calm. Then I remembered. That morning, the door to the cellar had been open, wide open. Rachel had fallen back through it and I had slammed it shut. I had never seen the door open all the time I had lived at the farm. In fact, it was grown over by long, matted grass and nettles. Had Rachel forced it open before she came into the cottage to attack me? Or had some unseen hand lifted the latch and pushed the creaking wood back on its hinges? Alice, were you watching over me?

I went to school the next morning and said nothing to anyone about my extraordinary weekend. I knew I looked pale and tired, and there were mauve-coloured rings under my eyes. At break there was a message from the secretary's office that I was wanted. With a feeling of dread I went along the corridor. Two policemen were jammed in amongst the filing cabinets and overflowing desks. They had removed their caps. One was nearly bald and had a rim on his forehead where his hat had left a mark. They were drinking cups of coffee and laughing with the two secretaries as I came in. They became more serious when they saw me.

Ridiculously I felt my heart beat faster and my colour mount. The women looked up, their faces full of ill-concealed curiosity. I wondered how much the police had told them. The bald officer suggested we find somewhere private to talk.

'Use the French classroom opposite,' said the older secretary, Mrs Roberts. 'It will be empty in break.'

We crossed the corridor and the gaggles of girls passing up and down gawped at us. I imagined the rumours which would be incubated and round the school in a

184

matter of minutes. So much for dealing with the attack with discretion. I felt very exposed and angry.

'You could at least have warned me you would come to the school,' I protested after I had shut the door. 'I should have told the headmistress that the police were likely to want to see me. God knows what everybody will think now. I had made up my mind not to tell anyone.'

The two officers looked unabashed. They had a job to do. The bald one was reaching into his top pocket for his notebook.

'Just a few things we needed to clear up with you, Miss Lennox. We won't keep you long. Mrs Pearson has made a full statement admitting that she entered your cottage on Sunday morning with the intention of attacking you with a plastic knife. We have had her sectioned under the Mental Health Act and she is now in the secure ward of a hospital in Basingstoke where she is undergoing assessment. She will remain there for at least three weeks. Meanwhile we need to establish whether you intend to press charges? If not, we can dispose of the case and pass it over to her doctor. Initially it seems that she is not a danger to the public and that this behaviour was totally out of character.'

'Okay,' I said, but I wasn't satisfied. 'How do I know she isn't going to do it again? Come and finish me off properly next time?'

'She will only be released if the doctors are confident that she is not a threat. We have spoken to her employers who have testified to her good character, although she has been a little unstable of late. Otherwise she has a completely clean record. Not even a parking ticket.'

'Who have you spoken to?' I asked sharply. 'Mr Mackintosh?'

'That particular gentleman was not available,' said the policeman laboriously. 'We spoke to another partner for whom Mrs Pearson now works. Mr Mackintosh, it seems, although still nominally Chairman, is semi-retired.'

'Where is he? Does he know what's happened? Has he been informed?'

The policeman shut his notebook; he had all he wanted. 'I can't comment on that,' he said. 'It wasn't necessary as part of police enquiries to speak to him personally, and I gather there is a certain amount of anxiety that this whole incident should be handled, er, sensitively . . .'

'Mmm. Yes, I bet,' I said. The two men looked at me sharply. I had again the strange feeling that somehow it was me in the wrong, me being judged. As if my rackety lifestyle had caused a lot of decent people a lot of trouble.

'Right,' I said. I had thought about the next bit. 'I don't want to press charges, but I do want to meet Mrs Pearson – Rachel. Can I do that? When she's better, of course. When the doctors think she's okay.'

The policemen looked at each other. 'We'll see what can be done. One of us will be in touch.'

They stood up and I took them out into the empty passage. The bell had rung for the end of break and there was no one to see them leave. However, Mrs Roberts was dithering about in the background waiting to catch me, to tell me that I was wanted for a moment in Mrs Anderson's office.

She led me back down the passage and I felt exactly like a naughty schoolgirl. I had hardly spoken to Mrs Anderson, the headmistress, since she had interviewed me for my job. Tall, grey-haired and imposing, she sat behind her desk and indicated I should sit on an armchair across from her. She said that she must demand some sort of explanation. She was astonished – no, outraged – that two police officers should enter her school to interview a member of staff. Again it was me who was put in the wrong. I felt myself blushing hotly.

'I'm terribly sorry,' I said. 'There was a sort of incident at the weekend. I was a witness and the police needed a statement. I told them they shouldn't have just turned up here. I had no idea they were coming. Of course, if I'd known I would have told you.'

'An incident?' she said coldly. 'What sort of incident and how were you involved in it?'

'I wasn't,' I said. 'I told you – I was a witness.' It was easier to lie than tell the unpalatable truth. 'If you don't mind, I'd rather not talk about it. Charges aren't going to be pressed and so you needn't worry about the newspapers or anything. The matter is closed now. Those policemen came here to tell me that.'

'I am glad to hear it. Nevertheless I would be obliged if you would explain to me more coherently the exact nature of what happened.'

'I can't,' I said. 'The police told me not to. For legal reasons.' A master stroke. I smiled and stood up. She still looked doubtful.

'I have a pupil waiting,' I said, 'and it's terribly important not to lose valuable teaching time, isn't it?'

When I got home that evening there was a large wodge of cellophane-wrapped flowers on the back doorstep. From Ned, I thought. However when I got them inside and onto the kitchen table, I opened the little envelope and the card inside bore a fat childish hand – the florist's, I supposed. *Darling*, it said. *What can I say? R.*

There was also a message from him on the answerphone. 'Sweetie, I'm shocked and horrified. Speak to you very soon.'

I unwrapped the flowers and shoved them in a bucket. I had no vase big enough to hold them. Later, I fished the broken cup out of the bin and spent the next half an hour sticking the handle pieces back together. I couldn't help it.

He could still move me to love him.

Chapter Sixteen

The week after what I thought of as my attempted murder, things seemed flat and uneventful. I felt strangely tired and listless. Ned must have sensed I needed space to sort things out and kept his distance. Robert telephoned as he promised. He was at home in Scotland for the rest of the summer. He had told Mary about the attack on me and it seemed she was not sympathetic. Why should she be? As for Rachel, he said, she had been his PA for fifteen years, he had slept with her on occasions when she had been very down, as he called it, after her divorce. She needed a little comfort, a shoulder to cry on. Her husband had treated her very badly. Robert had always thought that she perfectly understood the terms upon which they were intimate. His company had now decided to terminate her employment. It was obviously quite impossible for her to return and she had agreed to take a generous early retirement package.

He was grateful that I would not be pressing charges. It meant the whole thing could be settled neatly and swiftly. He was calm and businesslike; there was no need to overdramatise, his tone seemed to suggest. The whole business was sordid . . . regrettable, not the sort of thing he wished to be involved in. Somehow he had managed to distance himself from the results of his infidelities and the wreckage he left behind. He had retreated to his Scottish stronghold from where poor, mad Rachel was an object of pity, a sort of Mrs Rochester figure.

Meanwhile, Mary had not only chosen to brave it out, but apparently also took some satisfaction in having a husband for the love of whom quite ordinary women ran amok. Robert said that he had had to give her some kind of explanation for the extraordinary situation he found himself in, and that she was now entertaining her girlfriends with an edited account of the goings-on. I could imagine her voice, amused and amusing: 'You've no idea of what was awaiting us when we got back from Italy. Poor Robert. I do feel quite sorry for him. The woman was totally besotted. Can't think why, frankly. He's given her no encouragement but you know what these menopausal PAs can get like when they become fixated. The girl? I don't know really. Some musician who threw herself at him. Became a frightful nuisance.'

As the long-suffering wife of this highly desirable man, she would feel her own status enhanced. Other, lesser women could fight over him, but he came back to heel when she whistled. No one need know of his chronic infidelity, or be given any hint of her pain. While she could gloss over the truth, she could survive.

And Helen? I had to ask. I had to know what had happened to her, my enemy.

Helen, I learned, had returned to his club the items he had left in her houses and dumped them with the porter. This included the deck shoes he wore on her boat and a pair of walking boots he was intending to use on a holiday she had booked, walking from Gstaad in the Swiss Alps. I felt a sense of admiration at this gesture. She was still very angry and believed he was making a dreadful mistake. She was, as far as he knew, already seeing another man. 'Helen does not let the grass grow under her feet,' he said ruefully.

190

'Talking of grass,' I said, 'I'd like to have seen *her* six feet under. You know that I would gladly have murdered her? I often thought about it. I can't bear her. I still can't.'

'God, you women,' said Robert, in rather a pleased voice. He liked the idea of being the cause of all this unleashed passion, so contained and cool himself. 'Anyway, darling, thank God you are all right. Listen, I've sent a little something in the post for you – put it towards a holiday. You need a break.'

'Thanks,' I said. I felt angry with him and dissatisfied with his handling of my murder. He was buying me off as his firm had done Rachel. I wished I hadn't mended his cup. He sounded oh so smug. Viciously, I imagined him farting in Mary's bed and wondered how long she would put up with him before he veered off again in search of other lustful friendships.

After the telephone call I ate nearly a whole packet of chocolate digestive biscuits. I bolted them one after the other, standing at the kitchen counter jamming them in my mouth and licking my milk-chocolatey fingers. I knew that my behaviour was unhinged, but I couldn't stop. I needed the anaesthetic that a bloated stomach brings. I wanted to loll about, full of food, feeling nothing. I was just about to stuff the last one in my mouth and was wondering what I was going to eat next, when there was a knock on the door, which was standing open, and Ned was looking in. I blushed crimson. There is nothing so humiliating as being caught eating. It's worse, I think, than picking one's nose. Thank goodness, he didn't seem to notice.

'How are you doing?' he said, coming in and kissing me on the cheek. He was wearing a battered check shirt with two buttons missing. I could see smooth brown belly in the gaps.

'I'm okay.' I managed to recover myself. 'What about you? Here, have the last biscuit.' We smiled at each other and he put his arms round me. It felt utterly natural to lay my head on his checked front. I didn't feel any sexual thrill, just the pleasure of physical contact with someone I liked very much.

During this period I found it hard to sleep. My head was full of raging thoughts which took over at night. I would fall asleep, exhausted, only to wake at three in the morning with a brain as clear and sharp as a razor. My life seemed relentlessly laid out before me in these bleak sleepless hours, all my weaknesses revealed. I felt lonely and afraid. Where was I going? What was my future?

Worst of all was the overwhelming and inescapable knowledge that Robert didn't really want me and that I had been an entirely disposable part of his life. I had completely underestimated the strength of his marriage, which up until now I had rather scorned and despised. All the joy I had stored away in memories of our times together was doused by this cold truth. When it came to it, he had extracted himself smoothly and cleanly. He had emerged unbruised, his ego enhanced. I had been cut out cleanly from his life, like a malignant growth, a sucker. I, on the other hand, felt as if I had been torn apart.

My feelings ranged from anger to despair, self-hatred to misery. I tried to remember how he had made me feel and to value the pleasure we had shared, but I couldn't. I could only feel the pain of rejection and the humiliation of having loved unwisely. In these dark hours I believed Poppy had been right, I had achieved nothing by running off to the country. For four solid days I ate out of misery and my shirts started to gape open and waistbands cut into soft flesh. This could not go on, I told myself in the sleepless nights. I was sliding into an abyss: I felt unloved and unlovable.

Pilgrim and the cottage saved me. The late spring

moved into a vivid green early summer and I walked miles and miles in the translucent evenings after school. I grew stronger and fitter and leaner, and the exercise helped mend my mind. I always returned calmer and more peaceful. I followed the old bridleways and drove roads which threaded the country round the farm. Bluebells were followed by pink campion and froths of parsley. On the downs the little chalk flowers sprang from the springy turf and skylarks throbbed in the skies.

Pilgrim loved it. He chased rabbits with thrilling bursts of speed, or walked companionably at my heels. I sometimes met other dog walkers but mostly had the world to myself. One evening I met Ned and his wild collie, Fly, and just as the light was going we climbed the ramparts of an Iron Age fort and watched the dark creep over the valley below. We sat in silence, a bit apart, neither of us ready to move any closer. I liked him very much, of that there was no doubt, but did not want to hitch my happiness to another man. I wanted to restore myself first, be strong on my own, like myself a little better. I wasn't ready to love again.

Ned was not forthcoming either. Unlike Toby who has a need to reveal himself and to know and be known, Ned is a private sort of man. This suited me. I didn't want to learn about his past, or see his interior scars. He has long, brown, sensitive hands – in fact, his whole appearance is brown, as if he has gypsy blood, and as we sat there on the hill, he reached over and took one of my hands in his and gently stroked my fingers. It was sweet and touching. He came home with me and we shared a bottle of wine and laughed and talked, but when he left he didn't kiss me. It was as if he could sense my fragile recovery and was treating me with loving patience.

Another time I met Jake, my lecherous neighbour at the village supper, who was out riding with his daughter. He was on an enormous brown horse, all foaming and sweaty. It was restless and would not stand still. He kept on jabbing at its mouth. He looked handsome and dangerous, like a nineteenth-century squire.

'Well, hello!' he said. 'If it isn't our beautiful violinist. Where did you disappear to? I've been looking for you ever since that village party.'

'Oh?'

'I'm not letting you go before you say you'll come and have dinner. Katie, ride on and open the wicket gate at the end there's a good girl.' His daughter scowled and trotted off. The pony leaving produced further frenzy in his horse. Pilgrim took refuge behind me and I was obliged to climb up a bank and be stung by nettles to get out of the way of its huge Morris-dancing feet.

'Well, when can you come for supper?'

'Any old time, really. I haven't much on.'

'Would that were true,' he smirked.

Oh God, I thought. Piss off, please.

'Lucinda's away next week. Come and have a little dinner with me. I'll take you somewhere nice – beyond the means of violinists.'

I smiled sweetly, thinking, Bastard, bastard, bastard. 'Well, no. I'm sorry. I'm rather off married men.'

'Don't be silly. I'm not suggesting anything improper.' He managed to sound scornful. 'Just a bit of fun.'

'Yeah. Of course. Look, this is all very *Tess of the D'Urbervilles* – but if you don't mind, I want to get a move on.'

'Daddeeee!' Katie was wailing from the gate. 'Come *on*! I can't hold it open all this time!'

Unperturbed, Jake smiled. 'Okay. But I warn you, I don't give up easily. Do you good, a bit of country fun.' He blew me a kiss and then allowed his horse to bound away after the pony. It was a very bottomy departure; Jake's bum gripped by tight breeches bounced above the horse's great round backside which, with lifted tail and lather between its thighs, it swung in my direction.

Oh, up yours! I thought wearily.

My garden then took over as part of my therapy. I dug and weeded and planted. I put sweet peas to climb up a willow frame and sweet-smelling stocks around the door where I sat with a drink in the evening. Most of them were eaten by slugs and snails, but I was undeterred. I invited Mike down for a long weekend. I dithered about explaining his presence to Ned, but in the end when I told him, he did not seem concerned. 'It's good for you to have company,' he said.

I warned him that I wasn't going to confide in Mike, that I wanted him to be the only one to know the true details of what happened.

'Of course,' said Ned. 'I understand.'

Mike and I had a comfortable, happy, domestic time. I had planned a little supper party and invited Ned and Nicky. I had never met her and now I felt I knew Ned, I wanted to know his sister too. Mike had got very keen on cooking and I had to ferry him in and out of the nearest town where he shopped with great enthusiasm in the Saturday market. He bought Dorset crabs and local cheese and a huge free-range chicken, and hummed and sang and swigged from a bottle of wine all afternoon in the kitchen, while I acted as scullery maid.

Our guests arrived in a rush at eight o'clock while Mike was still wearing a tea towel tied round his middle with a bit of baler twine and was hot and pink from peering into saucepans. He had allowed me to go and have a bath and I felt cool and happy as I poured drinks. Nicky was tall and thin with the same shiny brown hair as her brother and the same self-contained, calm air. Mike got on really well with her and she went and chatted to him in the kitchen. Afterwards Ned said it was the first time he had seen her so relaxed and happy for ages and Mike told me that when she walked in, his heart stopped. I didn't believe people our age really could feel that, but he said it was

195

true and that it had never happened to him before.

Later, Nicky leant her elbows on my table and laughed and laughed at some of the absurdities which came out as the evening deteriorated into drunken confessions. Mike told us that his mother was known as the fastest woman in Shropshire, not only because she always won the mother's race at his prep school but because she ran off with so many fathers. He said that at the end of each term she would pick up a different selection of children, depending on who she was currently living with. It was dreadful, he said for him, as her only biological child, never knowing who he was going to spend the holidays with. This moved us girls to get up and kiss him, sloppily.

I had invited Toby as well and he brought a girl named Sophie, whom he called 'Soph' or 'Sophers', who had recently taken over as estate secretary. Although she enunciated like a duchess and had, as Toby called it, a booming forty-acre voice, she was really good fun. She was divorced with two small children. Her husband had run off with her best friend. 'They deserve each other,' she said.

Toby asked Mike to join the Sardinian party as he was short of people to fill the vast villa he'd booked. Mike agreed, and so did Nicky and Ned. I felt really happy and as if life was full of promise as I beamed round my kitchen table at my new, good friends. The picture they made, if freeze-framed, looked like a vision of a settled, enviable life; candles and bottles on a scrubbed table, an enamel jug full of flowers from the garden. Pilgrim asleep on his beanbag by the stove. We didn't look like flotsam . . . washed up, discarded, all misfits in a paired-up world. I didn't think about Robert once that evening. My Robert thoughts visited me at dawn.

So self-absorbed was I that first half of the busy summer term that I had not seen Caroline for some weeks. One evening I stopped on my way home from work and rang the doorbell of her house. It looked empty and shut up, and I was just turning to go when I heard a door close inside and footsteps. Caroline's mother, Geraldine, opened the door. She looked exhausted. Her hair was untidy and she had hastily drawn lipstick across her mouth.

'Oh, it's you,' she said, without smiling.

'How's Caroline?' I asked.

'Come in,' she said, standing back so I could move past her. She led the way into an immaculate kitchen which looked as if no meal had ever been cooked in it.

'Would you like a drink?' she said.

'Well, thank you. Yes. Is she okay?'

Geraldine opened a walk-in drinks cupboard in the far wall. She sloshed gin over ice and I heard the tonic fizzing. She turned back to me with two large tumblers and went to the counter to cut up a lemon.

'No,' she said, 'she's not.' She did not look up. 'She's in hospital. If she's doesn't improve very soon she will be dripfed. She has lost all inclination to save herself. As far as I can see, she is determined to die.'

I felt the savagery of her words smite me. They hung between us in the still air like knives.

'Oh God!' I said. 'I'm so sorry.'

'Yes. We're all sorry. Actually I'm angry too. I'm so angry with her that when I go to see her I want to hurt her. I want to force food down her mouth. I want to smack her. I'm finding it hard to cope with how I feel. My husband has gone to pieces. He's left me, actually. He's moved into a flat in London. She's in a specialist unit, you see. In London. I'm not allowed to see her. I, it seems, am the root cause of her illness.' She drained her gin and moved to pour another.

'My God!' I said. 'Don't say such things. I'm sure it's not your fault. She can get better, I'm sure she can. Can I see her? Would I be allowed to?'

'I've no idea. I don't believe at the moment she's allowed anyone. Visitors are used as a reward, you see. She has to earn them.'

'What happened at the place in Bristol? She was doing okay there, wasn't she?'

'Yes, she was, for a while. But then it started again – the vomiting, the lying, the manipulating. In the end they couldn't cope with her as a day patient. She had to be admitted into a ward.'

'I'm so terribly sorry.'

'In a way if she dies it will be a release. I've faced it, you see. I can't see any other way out. But she is strong; her body is strong. It's going to take a long time for her to kill herself – especially when they put the tubes in. She lies there with her face like a mask, full of hostility. She is a stranger. Of course, it's destroying us as well. She is getting what she wanted.'

My eyes filled with the tears that come too easily. I shook my head in disbelief and horror. I couldn't think of anything to say to this bitter, grieving woman. 'If there's anything I can do . . .' was the best I could manage. I finished my drink.

'Yes. Well, thank you.' Geraldine's face was set, as stubborn and fixed as her daughter's. No wonder her husband couldn't cope with this wall of anger and frustration and terrible pain. Her second gin slid back after the first. 'Can you see yourself out?' As I left the room, she was back into the cupboard and I heard the clink of ice.

I drove home moved to tears. Caroline, Caroline, I thought. What is locking you into self-destruction? What has pushed you to want to starve to death? What awful sickness has got inside your head to make you hate yourself to death?

I didn't know the answers and couldn't begin to imagine what demons occupied her mind, but I knew they were the product of the same sort of feelings I struggled with. Self-dislike, fear of rejection, fear of losing control, fear of life, but in her case, grown so large that they had taken her over. The mechanism which stopped me tipping over the edge, saved me from sliding into that hole, brought me back to normality, restored a balance in my life, seemed in Caroline to have jammed and failed to respond.

I telephoned Loops and told her.

'Oh shit!' she said. 'Where is she? Do you think I could go and see her? I really took to the kid. I'd like to help her if I could. She's been to see me a couple of times, but then I was out of London . . . and what with one thing and another, I lost touch. Oh God, I feel awful about that. Poor, poor kid.'

'Loops, so do I. Do you know, I haven't rung her or anything for weeks. In a way I was glad it had all gone quiet. I took it to mean she was getting on okay. I don't suppose I'd have made any difference but I wish I'd cared enough to find out how she was. I've been so wrapped up in myself.' I gave her what information I could and she promised she would ring the clinic.

'It's a hard, hard road to recovery, but she can get there. I've seen my friends on that road. When you are forced to eat, your body often takes over, takes back control. God, I hope it happens that way for her,' said Loops. We both fell silent, thinking of the other hideous resolution.

'Listen,' said Loops, changing the subject. 'I've given up that photography idea and I'm going to university instead. Yeah, amazing, isn't it? Me, who can't spell anything. It seems dyslexia doesn't matter any more. I'm doing a science degree at UCL, starting in October. I suddenly couldn't stand not using my brain. I've got science A-Levels, so it seemed sort of obvious. Eventually I'd like to do something para-medical, I think – psychotherapy or something. Anyway, I'm really excited about it. Can't believe it really, I hated fucking school.'

I made amazed and encouraging noises.

'Are you going out with someone new?' I asked, wondering if there was some fresh influence in her life.

Loops snorted down the phone. 'Funny you should ask. One of the blokes who interviewed me . . . an American professor called Dan Chomolski . . . I've been seeing him. He's a nice guy – a bit different from my usual sort. Short, hairy, Jewish. Shaped a bit like an egg. I've discovered how sexy a brain is. I'll bring him down to see you. How about you?'

I told her about Robert. Not about my murder. I didn't want to share that even with Loops, just about my unceremonial dumping.

'Good,' she said. 'Now you can get yourself a life, baby.'

'Actually I'd like to get a baby in my life.'

'You will one day. And at least it won't be that bastard's.'

Poppy was equally unequivocal.

'About time. He was one of your worst decisions, Hats. I mean, what was in it for you? An occasional bonk in return for not very much. You'd have done just as well with a long-distance lorry driver.' She seemed to have forgotten her role in the affair.

'Now I think we need to build you a portfolio of men,' she went on. 'I can think of one or two good long-term investments I can introduce you to, and then you'll need some short-term interests just to have a bit of fun with and cash in when they look like going down in value. Really, I think you should move back to London.'

'Pops, forget it. I'm not interested in the man market at the moment, and I really like it down here. I've made friends with some cool people.'

'Well, I'm coming down to see you. We need to consult diaries. I want you to come to Cornwall with me this summer. You, me, Jess and Tom . . . buckets and spades. But first we're going to celebrate your return to sanity. I'm on my way. My trainer has cancelled,' Poppy was now on a running and fitness regime, 'so I can come this afternoon. I'll be there when you get back from work.'

And she was. She turned up in the late afternoon in an artfully ragged lace skirt and silk flip-flop sandals with the children strapped into the back of her enormous shiny car. It seemed she had brought the entire contents of an Italian deli with her and two bottles of champagne, which we drank under the apple blossom while Jess amused herself trying to make Pedro wear a baseball cap and sunglasses and Tom sat, like a square, smiling bookend on a blanket. Poppy told me that amongst their friends the violin was becoming the most fashionable instrument for children to learn.

'It's easy to throw into the back of the car when one leaves Fulham for the country cottage and it doesn't distort the face, which of course is the problem with wind instruments. It's always better to have the most attractive child in the orchestra.'

I told her that I was doing very nicely out of private lessons and for the first time in my life had cleared my overdraft.

She was also more charitable about my teaching career. She now considered it less of a dead-end. She'd heard my school mentioned favourably by some new smart friends who were moving out of London to Wiltshire and were looking for somewhere to send their daughters.

'You're going to be all right, Hats. I feel much more confident about you. But you do need a man. I'm sorry, but if you go on drinking like this,' she waved her glass about, 'and living alone with this frightful dog,' she poked Pilgrim with her foot, 'you'll be an eccentric old dear in a few years, in a wonkily buttoned-up cardigan with stains down the front.' She looked at my current clothes. 'God, you're halfway there already.'

I scooped up Tom. He was a heavy, roly-poly lump in my arms. He put out his little dimpled hands and pulled my hair.

'Can I have a timeshare of Tom and Jess? Just to keep me going for the time being?'

'Of course, darling,' said Poppy, suddenly kind. 'Tom, don't suck Harriet's shirt. God knows where it's been.'

Later that same evening my mother and Douglas came over. My mother has always been fond of Poppy and loves her children whom she treats in a calm and firm manner, unlike my swooping and kissing and tickling. She sat with Poppy under the tree, discussing education which was now Poppy's almost sole topic of conversation while Douglas and I wandered about the garden. I showed him my attempts at flowerbeds and plantings and he was interested and kind.

You are a nice man, I thought. I watched him glance back from time to time to where my mother sat, composed and still, listening to Poppy rave on excitedly. He really loved her, I could see. We walked a little way down the farm track behind the cottage. Douglas had been silent for a while. He coughed and said, 'Harriet, I want you to know how happy we are. You and your sister and brother have been generous in welcoming me into the family and I want you to know how much I love your mother. I have to say, I never believed that this sort of happiness would come my way again. To tell you the truth, I have never felt like this before. The first time, with Margaret, was different. We didn't have this time together, the peace, the companionship which your mother and I share.'

'Douglas, I'm really glad. I can see she's happy.'

He looked uncomfortable. He had found it hard to talk in this vein. 'I just wanted you to know. In case you were wondering,' he finished lamely.

We walked back together in silence and he went and

stood behind my mother's chair and very lightly rested a hand on her shoulder. She looked up at him and smiled and covered his hand with her own. It was a tender moment and I was disturbed to feel a pang of my old jealousy. I stooped down to collect up the tea mugs from the grass to hide my brimming eyes and stumped off into the kitchen. Of course I was happy for them. I really was. I just wished that it was me.

Chapter Seventeen

After they'd all gone and I was washing up in the kitchen, I realised that this all-round condemnation of Robert had shifted my feelings. I felt almost defensive of him. Poppy and Loops were right in many ways, but they talked about him as if he had happened to me, like a disease, like something unpleasant I had caught. To save my feelings and bolster my recovery, they ignored my active role in our affair. They talked as if I was an innocent victim. Foolish, deluded, but basically misused.

This ignored the fact that it was me who had initiated our affair and me who had been desperate to continue. I had made all sorts of decisions along the way which had contributed largely to where I now found myself. I had to take at least equal responsibility for what had happened. Of course, I couldn't have known that I was likely to be attacked by a madwoman, but I did know that Robert was a chronically unfaithful man. I had assumed he would be different with me, that I was in some way special and more deserving than the other women in his life.

I found that I couldn't demonise Robert. He was exactly the same man I had been in love with. He hadn't changed. It was me who now saw things differently. I realised it was a relief to be free, to have untangled the web of dishonesty and deceit and feel it drop away. All the sticky strands which had caught and held me prisoner for so long seemed to have dissolved. What I felt for him now, I realised, was not bitterness or any desire for revenge. Nor, thank God, was it love. I suppose I could call it a mild affection. Christ, how that would annoy him! He liked his women passionate.

All this sounds strong and fine, but I have to admit that I only felt like this in my stronger moments; as yet I hadn't acheived a permanent recovery. There were times when I still longed for a telephone call, when I nursed hopes that he would come back to me when life with Mary assumed its habitual dullness. Several times I had to restrain myself from telephoning him. But I did so and as the days slid by I began to be at peace with myself for the first time in five years.

I also thought about Helen. I had a strong urge to contact her, as if a dialogue between us would some-how bring things to a close. Partly I felt the unity of wronged women: I wanted to align myself with her because she had also been discarded. I very nearly lifted the telephone to dial the number I knew by heart, but something stopped me. What was the point? The thread that held us together was gone. My feelings for her were an offshoot of my passion for Robert. With that displaced, Helen, too, was diminished. She wasn't important any more.

My visit to Rachel took place two days later, just before she was due to be released from the mental unit. I had fixed it up through the police, who were less than helpful. They had offered me something called victim support which I had turned down. I knew very well that in order to lay this particular ghost to rest I had to talk to Rachel. They seemed to feel this was inappropri-ate and were slow to disclose where she was or how I could gain admittance. In the end I rang the hospital direct and spoke to the psychiatric doctor who was looking after her. He had a sing-song Indian accent and was helpful and kind. It seemed that a chance to talk to me would in fact be a useful part of his rehabilitation programme and he rang me back later to say that Rachel had agreed to see me.

I didn't tell anyone where I was going. I stopped on the way – the hospital was in a horrible wasteland of ring roads and roundabouts on the outskirts of Basingstoke – and bought a bunch of flowers from a florist in an unpleasant arcade of modern shops. The flowers were pretty – a summer collection of mauve and white stocks whose heady scent filled the car. They looked as if they had been picked in a peaceful cottage garden.

The hospital was not hard to find but I sat in the visitors' car park for some time feeling nervous and afraid. I was glad that I had dear Pilgrim on the back seat. If I closed my eyes I could see Rachel's face distorted with hatred. I wondered if I had made a mistake in coming, if I could really bear to confront her and if it would do any good if I did. Eventually I got out, locked the car and walked to the door.

The hospital was housed in a flamboyant Edwardian mansion which sprouted new wings and annexes from all sides. I explained who I was at reception and was told to wait in a room lined with plastic and metal armchairs and tatty out-of-date magazines. There was no one else waiting. After a short while I heard steps approaching and a young Asian man came in. He wore casual clothes and trainers. He introduced himself as Rachel's psychiatrist and shook my hand. He had careful polite manners. He explained that Rachel had suffered a breakdown in layman's terms and that her extraordinary behaviour was unlikely ever to be repeated. She had completed all the necessary stages of recovery and expressed deep remorse for what she had done. She was very nervous about meeting me, but Dr Rajaphur felt, like me, that a meeting would be mutually beneficial. If I was ready he would take me to her. We would be left alone together but at all times the door would be open and staff at hand. 'You are at no risk,' he kept repeating, which made me feel all the more nervous.

He then led the way through a series of locked and coded doors and then into a lift and up two floors. The corridor we entered was strangely quiet and dreamlike. Were all the patients drugged, I wondered. He showed me into a small room which had been clumsily carved from a much larger one. The ceiling was very high and an elaborate cornice was truncated by the dividing wall. A big metal radiator belted out heat although the day was warm and the room was stifling. The scent of the stocks now struck me as sickly and overwhelming. The high window was also divided, so that half was in the next door room. It was hung with venetian blinds which gave a slashed view of the car park outside. It felt mad, peculiar, as if the outside world had been disconnected. Two armchairs faced one another with a round coffee table between. On the walls were two stylised paintings of yachts, slicing at an angle through blue waves. The colours were hectic and hard.

Dr Rajaphur left me for a minute and then I heard him returning, he was talking to someone in a low voice. It was Rachel, looking smaller, more fragile, older. We stared at one another and then in a rush she took my hand and held it between hers. Her voice was very soft and quiet and her words came in little breathy rushes.

'What can I say? Oh! I'm so, so sorry for the terrible thing I did.'

'It's okay,' I said. 'I'm perfectly all right, although I have to say I was bloody frightened at the time.'

I smiled and she smiled tentatively back. Her skin was very pale and paperlike, criss-crossed with fine lines. She looked older than fifty. Her hair was thin and dark and hung limply round her face. She had rinsed it with an ugly metallic copper colour. Her eyes were a pretty violet blue but they were full of pain. I tried to imagine Robert with her, his great weight bearing down on her, his meaty face hanging over hers.

'Are you thinking of him?' she asked.

'Yes, I was, actually. But not very flatteringly. Can we talk about him? Do you mind?'

'No, I don't mind. Since I've been in here, and the treatment and the pills, I feel I can cope with it. What do you want to know? It's obvious that I loved him. You see, I loved him so much. I've loved him since the first week I worked for him. He was my ideal man. When I went through my divorce, which in a way I can see was because of him, although I denied it at the time, he became – well, more affectionate towards me. He only slept with me three times. He explained about his wife and family and so on, and I accepted that. What I couldn't bear was when I knew he had other women . . . a whole string of them. I used to hear him on the telephone, see him come back flushed from an afternoon in bed. I had to deal with their telephone calls, sometimes even post his letters to them. He's a great letter-writer. He likes to while away his time in the office writing to his women. I hated you most of all because I could tell that you were young. I thought you had more control over him than the others, more of a hold. He was on the point of retiring so I knew I was going to lose him anyway and I had sort of held out a hope that he might keep me on as a lover. But you finished that. I hated you so much. I imagined you carelessly accepting his love. I didn't think you were good enough. I saw a photo of you. Do you know the one? He kept it in his desk drawer. It was of you on a beach in rolled-up jeans and his sweater with your long blonde hair blowing across your face.'

'That wasn't me,' I interrupted. 'I've never had a photo taken like that. I've never been on any beach with him.'

'Well, anyway, I thought it was. I found out where

you worked and then where you lived. I got so I couldn't stop thinking about you. I thought he was with you all the time. I kept ringing just to hear your voice. I often drove down to your cottage at weekends and just drove round and round. I've passed you in your lane three or four times. You had to reverse to let our cars pass. I've sat in the pub behind you while you were having lunch with your other boyfriend. I've followed you round Salisbury. I was in the same changing room when you were trying on clothes in Bath just after Christmas. I saw your big breasts and your sexy figure and I'm afraid I pictured you in bed with him and I knew that he would never look at me again. He used to call my breasts "bee stings". He called me "Skinny Lizzie". I suppose I became more and more unhinged. I was going through a very difficult menopause. The final straw came when he told me he was returning to Mary fulltime. Of course, I didn't believe him. I thought he was saying it as a way out. I thought he was going off with you. That's when I told Helen. That's why she planned your murder. Of course, I couldn't do it for real. I only took a toy knife. She'd told me to use a breadknife.'

I gaped at Rachel. *Helen* was involved in this?

'My God, I had no idea. Helen! Robert swore she didn't know about us. Have you told the police this?'

'Yes, of course. They said they had tried to contact Helen but she is out of the country. I don't think they believed that she suggested I do it. Or at least, not seriously. They didn't seem to think it was important.'

'But of course it is! It is to me, anyway. She wanted me dead. Why aren't the police interested? Doesn't it make her an accomplice or an accessory or something?'

'No, I don't think so. She never really commanded me to kill you. When I said how much I hated you and that I was sure you were behind the business about going back to Mary, Helen said something like: "God, I could kill her. Well, why don't you? You feel the same. Stab the bitch with a breadknife. You'd be doing us both a favour." '

'God! Charming! I can't really believe this. Do you think she realised, sorry but I don't know how to put this . . . did she realise how unstable you were at the time? Did she think that you just might try and kill me?'

'I don't know – I only talked to her twice. She suggested I catch you on a Sunday morning. She said you'd be sure to have a lie-in . . . to catch your dog and slip in while the door was open. She said I'd take you totally by surprise.'

'Wait a minute. How did she know all this about me? How does she know I have a dog and what I do on Sunday mornings?'

Rachel looked at me, surprised. 'She knew already, before I told her. She'd found out, been down to your cottage, I think. Watched you.'

I felt a wave of nausea. Robert's assurances that Helen suspected nothing had made me feel secure and safe, and all the time my life had been as fragile as a house of cards. How little he knew his women.

I covered my face with my hands. 'I can't bear this. It's too horrible. Too frightening. How did she find out about me? How long has she known?'

'Not long. She said that she had been away with Robert, and that he wrote postcards to you all the time. It made her furious. When they got back she was determined to find out about you. But you needn't worry about Helen. If you haven't got Robert, she's not interested in you. She thought you were only a minor player anyway.'

'A minor player?' I now felt as insulted as I did frightened.

'Yes. She didn't think you represented much of a threat. A passing fancy, I think she called you. A "bit of fluff". She thought she could see you off. I pointed out that you had youth on your side – that you made him laugh, feel young again. Remember I'd seen it happen, watched him come back from being with you. I saw how good you made him feel.'

Thank you for that, Rachel, I thought. Stupidly, stupidly, I felt pleased, and glad that Helen had been made to think again.

'I had been watching you for some time, you know,' said Rachel. 'I had tried to get into your cottage before, but that other woman was always there.'

'What other woman?'

'That woman who lives with you. About forty, short, with dark hair. Twice she was in the garden. She looked straight at me and I had to drive on. Once she opened the door and just stood there. She never said a word.'

Loops? Could it be Loops?

'Are you sure she wasn't tall and fantastically beautiful?'

'No. She was a homely-looking woman. She had a long dress on, and an apron.'

Then suddenly I knew. It was Alice.

A nurse brought us orange-coloured tea in heavy thick cups.

'Do you still love him?' I asked Rachel. 'What is it about him anyway? How has he done this to us all? You, me, Helen.'

Rachel considered. 'I have been so drugged in here that I don't really feel anything at the moment, but the awful thing I did has finally brought me to my senses. I think I will always love him, but I'm going to let it go now, stop it possessing me. I must accept it for what it was . . . a fleeting affair.'

She, so far, had expressed no interest in me or my relationship with Robert. Love makes one extraordinarily self-centred, I thought.

212

'Can I tell you a bit of this from my point of view?' I began. 'So that you can put me in my proper place in this story. Robert never loved me, not for one moment. He made that clear at the beginning and it was true right through to the end. In fact, I'm not sure he's capable of love. I think he would find it too uncomfortable and disturbing. Do you think any of us have given him a sleepless night? I doubt it. Anyway, as I got more involved I wanted more of him. And then I found out about Helen and it upset me a lot. I couldn't bear sharing him and she seemed to have all the advantages. I didn't know about you. I don't think he actually misled me, he just never felt the necessity for me to know. We were all compartmentalised, weren't we? It seems he always finds women who are needy in some way . . . he sees it like providing a service. It makes him able to justify his behaviour and, in fact, feel quite good about himself. Poor Helen having a terrible time with her husband. Poor Rachel married to a bastard. Poor Harriet reaching thirty and no man. Anyway, I've slowly woken up to the fact that my affair with him was costing me a great deal more than it did him, and I felt I deserved more. I want more than a drop-in lover. When he told me it was coming to an end I felt quite equivocal about it. Oh yes, I had bad moments, but I always did with him, right from the start. It was never undiluted bliss, was it? But I imagined it was with Helen. I thought she had the best of him. In the end I hated Helen more than I loved him.'

'I don't think they were like that,' said Rachel. 'They argued a lot. She was always trying to arrange a life for them. She wanted him as an escort, to show him off. Of course he couldn't risk that. Helen and I thought you had everything in your favour. Youth for one thing – that's what Helen couldn't bear. And Robert is adept at the most crushing of personal remarks, isn't he? He was always reminding Helen of how good-looking she'd been once. And I was so stupid and blind, I thought I could keep him. If I was loyal and faithful and always available, then, in a very small way, when he was in London, he might want me . . . remember the times we had together.' She looked as if she was going to cry. She was rubbing at her mouth with frantic hands. I glanced round nervously. I hoped there really was someone out there if she was going to go over the top. I couldn't face another scene.

'He's been bad for us all, hasn't he?' I said quietly. 'For you, for me, for Helen. He told me he was sending me a cheque, although it hasn't arrived. I pictured him and Mary deciding an appropriate amount. And you've been paid off, I believe. He thinks he has squared things off neatly and behaved quite generously. After all, he'll tell himself, we always knew the ground rules. He was always honest with us.'

'Yes. We're fools. Fools to accept those terms. But, if I'm honest, I'd have had him on any terms.'

'Tell me more about Helen. God, she's occupied a lot of my thoughts, I can tell you. What's she like?'

Rachel considered. 'Fiftyish. Smart. Very well-groomed. Hard, I should think. Likes to get her own way.'

'Beautiful?'

'No. Face like a hatchet. Big chin. Sharp nose. Sharp teeth.'

We both laughed.

'You're much prettier,' she said. I loved her then. It was what I wanted to hear. I didn't care if it was true or not.

'Look, I brought you these.' I passed her the flowers. 'And I just wanted to wish you well and to say that as far as I am concerned, this is all in the past. Frankly, I want to put it behind me and get on with life. There's one thing, though. We ought to promise each other that there's no going back, however seductive, whatever he says or does.'

Rachel looked at me sharply. 'Why, do you think he'll get in touch with me? Has he said anything to you?' Her voice had a lift of hope. My words were useless. I could see she was irredeemably lost. I smiled and shrugged a non-committal answer, and stood up to leave.

So, Alice, I thought as I drove home. Alice, you guarded me. I did not want to look for any other logical explanation for the woman Rachel had seen. So sure was I that when I unlocked the door of Jerusalem Farm and stood in my sunny kitchen I said out loud, 'Thank you, Alice, for watching over me.' The cottage creaked above me, as it often does when the old timbers shift and strain. It sounded as if someone was walking softly across the upper floor. Alice, I knew, was waiting at the top of the stairs to welcome me back.

⊶

I found Alice's grave in the churchyard the other day. She shares a headstone with her husband and three of her children. There she was under her husband's name: *and also* it read, *his wife, Alice, aged 33*. I laid my hand on the old stone which was covered in hard little blooms of orange lichen. The churchyard was peaceful and still. Rooks cawed in the trees along the road and there was the usual noise of bleating sheep – sounds that hadn't changed in a thousand years. The grave was now just a rounded hump of grass which the mower could sweep over.

You are not just an 'also', Alice, I thought. Oh no. Your strength and courage held your little family together. Six times you went through bloody childbirth and the cottage rang with your screams while the other children were sent into the yard to get them out of the way. You nursed and fed and clothed those children, watched your young husband die, faced a bleak future on your own. You scrubbed and polished and swept those rooms, dug that garden, cursed the fire which is so hard to light. You felt your strength ebbing that last winter when you gave the children your share of bread and lay coughing through the night. No wonder your spirit is still there, unable to rest.

The last scene I found almost too painful to contemplate . . . the cart winding up the hill from the village, the few possessions stacked by the door and heaved on by the carter, followed by the children. Last of all little Lucy, just three, miserable, whimpering for her mother, unable to understand that she had forsaken them, gone for ever, laid out cold and stiff in the bedroom with her heart broken at the leaving of them. The cart would start off, along the same lanes I walked now, creaking on its way to Shaftesbury and the Poor House. Alice left for ever to move through the rooms of Jerusalem Farm, restless and grieving.

My thoughts were broken by the children let out of the village school. They streamed down Cowpath Lane, chattering and laughing, running ahead of their brightly dressed young mothers, swarming round the shop, clamouring for sweets.

Ned, who had been in the shop to buy a newspaper, waited for me on the seat by the church gate, Fly panting by his feet, Pilgrim standing, watching me anxiously. I had to go.

'Alice,' I said, 'it's time to rest. Sleep well, my friend.' And I left her a little posy of the lavender which grows by the back door of the farm, and rosemary too. Rosemary for remembrance.

As I turned away, Ned stood up and came to meet me at the gate with Fly swarming around his legs.

'Last respects?' he asked gently, opening the gate for me.

'Yes,' I said. I was grateful that he let me feel how I did about Alice without suggesting I was mad or fanciful. He put his arm round my shoulders, and we walked back across the green towards the lane to the farm.

Pilgrim nudged my hand with his long nose and I caressed his slippery, velvet ear with my fingers.

'Helen, too,' I said. 'She's gone as well, Ned. Laid to rest.'

Ned nodded, saying nothing, but giving my arm a squeeze.

It was a lovely afternoon. The sun sent spools of swimming golden light through the trees, and the lane foamed with creamy cow parsley. As we climbed the hill and rounded the last bend, there was Jerusalem Farm, snug in the shoulder of the land. I loved approaching it like this, on foot, watching the cottage slowly appear in the distance as if it was sitting there, waiting for us. I let Pilgrim off his lead and he raced on ahead, chased by Fly.

'He knows his way home,' said Ned, and I realised how glad I was to hear those words. Home for Pilgrim and home for me. We had both come a long way, it seemed, but we had reached home at last.